ZONDERKIDZ

Adventure Bible Handbook
Copyright © 2013 by Robin Schmitt and David Frees
Illustrations © 2014 by Craig Philips

This title is also available as a Zondervan ebook.
Visit www.zondervan.com/ebooks.

Requests for information should be addressed to:

Zonderkidz, *Grand Rapids, Michigan* 49530

ISBN 978-0-310-72575-6

Scriptures taken from the Holy Bible, *New International Reader's Version®, NIrV®.*
Copyright© 1995, 1996, 1998 by Biblica, Inc.™ Used by permission of Zondervan.
All rights reserved worldwide.

Editor: Kim Childress
Art direction and design: Mike Harrigan, MotionDrone

Printed in China

13 14 15 16 17 /DSC/ 10 9 8 7 6 5 4 3 2 1

A Wild Ride Through the Bible

ADVENTURE BIBLE HANDBOOK

 ZONDERkidz

THE GARDEN OF EDEN

In the beginning God created the heavens and the earth (Genesis 1:1). The earth was formless, and God decided to create a paradise in this place. He created night and day, land, water, plants, and animals. Next he created mankind. The first people were Adam and Eve. God gave Adam and Eve a beautiful garden to live in—Eden. Eden had food, water, shelter, and everything Adam and Eve needed. God asked Adam and Eve to take care of the garden, and God visited and walked through the garden with them.

I DON'T BELIEVE IT! WE'RE IN THE GARDEN OF EDEN. AND LOOK! THERE'S ADAM AND EVE! WOW, IT'S NICE AROUND HERE. THEY'VE REALLY GOT IT MADE.

DIDN'T I TELL YOU THESE TOUR GUIDES WERE INCREDIBLE?

WON'T WE MESS UP THE SPACE/TIME CONTINUUM? THE WHOLE FABRIC OF THE UNIVERSE COULD UNRAVEL!

NO, NO. THAT'S JUST A BUNCH OF SCI-FI MUMBO JUMBO. IN REAL LIFE, WHEN YOU TRAVEL THROUGH TIME AND SPACE, YOU'RE IN A KIND OF TIME-WARP BUBBLE

NOBODY CAN SEE YOU, AND YOU CAN'T AFFECT ANYTHING THAT HAPPENS. OR HAPPENED. OR WILL HAPPEN.

ANYWAY, JUST REMEMBER TO KEEP YOUR RSP WITH YOU. IF YOU LOSE IT, YOU COULD BE STUCK HERE FOREVER.

EFFECTS OF SIN ON CREATION

Taking a bite of the fruit forbidden, which Adam and Eve were told not to eat, doesn't seem like a very big deal – but it was. The result of doing what God had told them not to do was a broken relationship between all people and the creator of the world.

We read in Genesis 2, the first book of the Bible, that God told Adam and Eve that they could eat from any tree in the Garden of Eden except for one tree, on which grew a unique type of fruit. Have you ever done something that you knew was wrong but did it anyway?

WHAT IS SIN?

Sin is either doing what God has told us not to do, or not doing what he has told us to do. An example is if you were told to not throw a ball in the house. Since you know the rule, it is your choice whether you follow the rule or choose to throw the ball. Even if nobody sees, and you throw the ball, you have still broken the house rule. This applies to God's laws, or rules. He has given us a set of rules to live our lives by, and when we break them, we sin.

THINGS HAVE GOTTEN GLOOMY AROUND HERE. WHAT SAY WE NAVIGATE TO THE SECOND STOP ON OUR TOUR AND SEE WHAT HAPPENS NEXT?

OKAY, TIME TO CALL IN THE CHOPPER!

YEAH, I DON'T THINK WE'LL FIND DAD HERE.

THE PROBLEM & THE SOLUTION

God told Adam and Eve that the punishment for eating the fruit from the one tree in the middle of the garden would cause them to die. Before this time nothing in the world had died. But once they had eaten the forbidden fruit, not only did they die spiritually, they began to die physically. The spiritual death was a separation between God and mankind.

The bite that Adam and Eve took from the forbidden fruit has continued to affect every person who is born. Adam and Eve disobeyed God and brought sin into the world. But because God still loved Adam and Eve, as well as all other people who would be born after them, he had to have a sacrifice to fix the problem.

THE GARDEN OF EDEN

Genesis 3:24 "After he drove the man out, he placed on the east side of the Garden of Eden cherubim and a flaming sword flashing back and forth to guard the way to the tree of life."

Many years after Adam and Eve's disobedience, people continued to misbehave. Adam and Even had two sons, Cain and Abel. Cain didn't like Abel (which isn't unusual for brothers to fight), so he killed him (which is overdoing it!). That was the first murder. The world kept getting worse. People forgot God and treated each other so poorly that God decided to start over. He decided to destroy the world and all people with a flood. Everybody, that is, except Noah and his family—and the animals God sent to Noah. Noah had remained faithful and true to God, so God sent instructions on building the great ark.

THE ARK

LENGTH: 450 FEET   **WIDTH:** 75 FEET   **HEIGHT:** 45 FEET

Noah's ark was twice as long as a Boeing 747.

DON'T WORRY, KIDS. THIS RAIN WON'T LAST FOREVER. PRETTY SOON THERE'LL BE BLUE SKIES AND A RAINBOW.

GOD IS RESCUING SOME GOOD PEOPLE AND A LOT OF ANIMALS. HE'S GIVING THE WORLD A SECOND CHANCE.

HANG ON, EVERYBODY. WE'RE HEADING FOR OUR NEXT STOP!

Noah obeyed God and started building the ark, even though his friends and others in his community laughed at him. When the ark was finished, God's word became true, and the flood came. God sent huge amounts of water that covered the earth. The rain lasted forty days and forty nights, but the water lasted 371 days. Noah spent one year and seventeen days in the ark with his family and the animals! (Can you imagine the smell?) Finally the water receded, and the ark landed on Mount Ararat. God made a promise to Noah that He would never destroy the world again by a flood. The symbol of this promise is a rainbow that can still be seen in the clouds today. (Genesis chapters 7-9)

Stories of the flood are found in the ancient traditions of the American Indians, Egypt, Greece, China, India, Mexico, Britain, and other places.

THE TOWER OF BABEL

Many years after the flood, a group of people in a place called Shinar decided to build a tower that would reach to the heavens. The tower was called Babel. Up until this time all the people of the earth spoke the same language. The people wanted to reach heaven so they could be like God. God didn't like this plan, so God caused the people to begin speaking in different languages. God caused confusion, and no one understood "pass me that peg and pulley." Building came to a halt. (Genesis 11:1-9)

LANGUAGES OF THE BIBLE

The words of the Bible were originally written in two languages. The Old Testament was written mostly in Hebrew. To us, Hebrew looks very strange. It's written backwards, from right to left. The New Testament was written mostly in Greek. Greek was the language almost everybody used in the time of Jesus, and it looks much more like English. Some of the stories of the Bible were written on tablets of clay, or dried animal skins, because paper had not been invented yet.

Because of the work of translators, the Bible has been translated into many different languages. Today, people from every part of the world can read the stories of the Bible in their own language. One of those languages is English, which you are reading now.

ABRAHAM

Abraham, or Abram, as he was once called, was told by God to leave the area where he had grown up and move to a new land called Canaan. This took a lot of faith and obedience on Abraham's part because he was leaving behind everything he knew. Abraham and his wife, Sarah, moved to Canaan as God had instructed. This move would take Abraham almost six hundred miles away from his family into an unfamiliar land. Abraham's journey to Canaan was part of God's plan for reconciling himself with mankind. (Genesis 12:1-20)

TRAVEL

Travel during the time of the Old Testament was not easy. There were no roads or cars. People either walked or rode an animal such as a donkey or camel. To make matters worse, most towns were days apart. Travel during this time was long, difficult, and dangerous. There were wild animals like lions and bears. There were bandits ready to attack and no police for protection. People traveled mainly at night to avoid robbers and because it was cooler. And the going was sloooow! Most travelers could only go about nine or ten miles a day. (That's like five minutes in a car.) And when people went on a trip, they had to bring enough food and water to make it to their next destination. If Abraham and his family could have gone straight, they would have only had to go about 600 miles. But they had to travel along the river because they needed water, so they went about 1,100 miles from Ur to Schechem. Today we could fly that amount in a few hours or drive it in a couple days. It took Abraham about four months!

POSSIBLE ROUTES OF ABRAHAM'S JOURNEY

Haran

Nineveh

Asshur

Damascus

Ramoth Gilead

Shechem   Succoth

Babylon

Ur

ABRAHAM'S FAMILY

Abraham grew up in a place called Ur of the Chaldeans. When he was older, his family moved to the land of Canaan. However, when they got to a town called Harran, Abraham's father (Terah) decided to stay. When Abraham grew up, he married Sarah. One day God came to Abraham and told him to leave Harran and go to the land of Canaan, which God promised to give him and his descendants. (Genesis 12:1-4)

There was only one problem with God's promise. Abraham and Sarah never had children. As they grew older Abraham and Sarah always followed God's commands. Because of their faithfulness, God made them another promise. God said he would give Abraham and Sarah a child (Genesis 15), and just as God had promised, Abraham and Sarah had a son. They called him Isaac. When Isaac was born, Abraham was one hundred years old, and Sarah was ninety!

It was through Isaac that God promised to bless all the nations. Isaac had two children, Esau and Jacob. Esau and Jacob were twins, but Esau was born first. In Old Testament times, the oldest son inherited everything, so Esau would inherit his father's possessions and receive a special blessing.

Jacob was jealous. One day Esau came home very hungry, and Jacob traded Esau's birthright for a bowl of beans! In spite of the sneaky way Jacob got his father's blessing, God also blessed Jacob, and in a dream, God promised that Jacob would become a large nation and a blessing to the whole world.

Jacob had twelve children. Jacob's twelve sons would later become the nation of Israel. As we read in the New Testament, we learn that it was through the line of Judah, one of Jacob's twelve sons, that King David and Jesus were born. Jesus was the ultimate fulfillment of God's promise to Abraham—that he would have many descendants and all nations would be blessed through him.

THIS WHOLE T-T-TOUR THING IS A B-B-BIG MISTAKE...

JACOB'S NAME CHANGE

The name Jacob means "to cheat." But in a dream, Jacob wrestled with God, and Jacob persevered. God gave Jacob a new name, Israel, which means "Prince of God." Abraham's descendants became known as Israelites, and the whole nation was called Israel.

THIS IS IT— CANAAN, THE LAND GOD PROMISED TO ABRAHAM AND HIS DESCENDANTS.

THAT'S WHY THEY CALL IT THE PROMISED LAND!

THAT TRIP DIDN'T TAKE AS LONG AS I EXPECTED.

ADVENTURE READINGS

Abraham and Lot: Genesis 13-14

Hagar and Ishmael: Genesis 16

Destruction of Sodom and Gomorrah: Genesis 18:1-33; 19:1, 12-29

Hagar and Ishmael are sent away: Genesis 21:8-20

God asks Abraham to sacrifice Isaac: Genesis 22:1-19

THANKS TO RSP TECHNOLOGY, WE GOT HERE A LITTLE FASTER THAN ABRAHAM DID. CAN'T WASTE TIME, YOU KNOW.

AND SPEAKING OF TIME, IT'S TIME TO DO A LITTLE TIME-JUMP BACK TO BIBLE TIMES. GET READY, EVERYONE!

CHECK THIS OUT. CAMEL SURFING!

JOSEPH & EGYPT

Of Jacob's twelve sons, Benjamin and Joseph were his two youngest. Before Benjamin was born, Jacob favored Joseph and gave him special privileges that his older brothers did not have. Because of Jacob's favoritism toward Joseph, Joseph's older brothers became resentful and angry with him. Once Joseph was given a coat from his father made from many colorful pieces of fabric. Though it was a wonderful gift, it again showed his brothers that their father liked Joseph best.

One night Joseph had a dream that his brothers were bowing down to him. When he told the dream to his brothers, they became very angry and wanted to kill him. A few days later, Joseph was sent by his father to check on his brothers who were out in the field. When they saw Joseph coming, they decided to throw him into a cistern, a type of well, and sold him to a group of traders who were passing by on their way to Egypt. To explain to their father why Joseph was missing, they poured some blood on his colorful coat and told their father that an animal had attacked and killed Joseph. Jacob was very sad, and Joseph was sold as a slave in Egypt. (Genesis 37:18-36)

EGYPT

Egypt is a very big country, although most Egyptians live along the Nile River. The river helps people grow food and travel from one city to another without too much work. During the time of the Old Testament, the Nile River would rise each year about twenty-four feet and flood the surrounding lands. At first you might think this is a bad thing, but the flood water contained needed nutrients that made the soil rich, which provided food for the people of the land. Many of the stories that you read about in Genesis and Exodus take place in this land of Pharaohs, pyramids, and sand. In fact, Egypt contains a lot of sand. Egypt is mostly a desert area, which is why most of the people live near the Nile River.

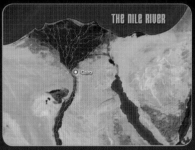

THE NILE RIVER

PYRAMIDS & ARCHAEOLOGY

The pyramids are large structures that are square at the bottom with a point at the top and were built in Egypt by slaves several thousand years ago—after the time Joseph lived. Many of these slaves were of Joseph's family and were called the Israelites. There are still some pyramids standing in Egypt today that can be visited—if you're willing to ride a camel to get to them.

ARCHAEOLOGY & MUMMIES

Archaeology is the study of items left behind by a culture to determine how they lived and what they believed. To find these items, archeologists carefully dig in the ground with hopes of finding pottery, jewelry, or even entire buildings. Through these finds, archaeologists try to piece together how the people lived and acted.

One practice archaeologists have learned about is how Egyptians preserved the bodies of those who died, a traditional ritual called mummification. Mummification is the process of taking the body of someone who has died and wrapping him up in strips of cloth before placing the body in a tomb. One example of a mummy that archaeologists have found is the body of King Tut. King Tut's mummified body was found in a burial room, or tomb, inside a pyramid. Archaeologists also found valuable items like gold, jewelry, and weapons, which the Egyptians believed would protect King Tut after his death.

JOSEPH'S JOURNEY IN EGYPT

After being sold to Potifer as a slave, Joseph worked hard and eventually became Potifer's property manager. In his new position, Joseph spent much of his time around the main house, where he met Potifer's wife. She did not like Joseph because he was an honorable man and would not do anything to hurt Potifer. She told her husband lies about Joseph that caused Joseph to be thrown in prison. (Genesis 39:1-18)

While Joseph was in prison, the Pharaoh became angry with two of his officials, a baker and a cupbearer, whom he had thrown into prison. One night both of the men had a strange dream. The next morning they discussed their dreams with each other, but they could not figure out what the dreams meant. Joseph, however, was able to interpret the meaning of their dreams and explain what they meant. Unfortunately, the meaning of the baker's dream was not good news. Joseph said it meant that he was going to die very soon. The cupbearer's dream was very good news, as Joseph said it meant that he was going to be back at his old job and continue working for Pharaoh. The results came about just as he had predicted. (Genesis 40:1-23)

Two years later, the Pharaoh had a strange dream about seven fat cows and seven skinny cows. No one in his court could explain these dreams to the Pharaoh. Then the cupbearer remembered his own dream and how Joseph had been able to explain it. Joseph was brought before the Pharaoh. Joseph explained that the cows represented seven years. The seven fat cows were seven good years for growing and harvesting crops and the seven skinny cows were seven bad years of bad crops and famine. The Pharaoh was impressed with Joseph and put him in charge of all the food supplies in Egypt.

Joseph not only helped to save Egypt from the years of famine, he also saved his brothers and their families. Like Egypt, Canaan's citizens, where Joseph's family still lived, were starving and in need of food. Joseph's brothers travelled to Egypt to ask for food. At first the brothers did not recognize Joseph, but later he revealed his true identity and saved his family and many others during the famine. (Genesis 41-43)

MOSES

Four hundred years after Joseph lived, there was a little boy who was born in Egypt during troubled times. The Pharaoh, who ruled at this time, mistreated the people of Israel. He was so mean that he gave an order demanding that all recently born baby boys were to be killed. One mother decided to try and save her son by placing him in a basket and letting him float down the Nile River. This little boy was Moses. Moses' sister, Miriam, followed the basket as it floated in the water until it reached the bathing spot of the Pharaoh's daughter. The Pharaoh's daughter found the baby and chose to take him and adopt him as her own son. Moses grew up as a grandson in Pharaoh's court.

Many years later, when Moses was about forty years old, he saw one of the Israelite slaves being beaten by an Egyptian guard. This angered Moses so much he struck the guard and killed him. Moses knew what he had done was wrong, so he fled Pharaoh's court and ran away to the land of Midian. Eventually Moses stopped running and took a job as a shepherd working for a man named Jethro. (Exodus 2:1-14)

THE PLAGUES

When Moses was about eighty years old, as he was out taking care of his sheep in a field, a voice spoke to him from a burning bush. Of course, it was not really the bush that was talking, but God. God simply used the bush to get Moses' attention. God told Moses to return to Pharaoh's court and tell him to let the people of Israel go. After some argument, Moses went to Egypt and told Pharaoh exactly what God had said. Unfortunately, Pharaoh refused to listen and began to turn his heart against God. Eventually, after several attempts to convince Pharaoh that God was serious, ten different plagues were sent to afflict the Egyptians.

THE PLAGUES WERE:

1. The water turning into blood
2. Frogs
3. Mosquitoes
4. Flies
5. Animals became sick and died
6. Boils
7. Hail
8. Locusts
9. Darkness
10. Death of the firstborn

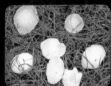

After each plague, Moses went back to Pharaoh and requested that he release the Israelites. But Pharaoh refused to release the people. In the last plague, in which Pharaoh's own firstborn child died, he realized he was powerless against the God of Moses and decided to let the people go. (Exodus 3, 6-12)

As the Israelites started their exit out of Egypt, which is why it is called the *Exodus*, they took with them items made of gold and silver that the Egyptians gave them. Under the leadership of Moses, there could have been as many as one million Israelites who left Egypt that day. Once all of the Israelites were gone, Pharaoh realized he had let all his workers go. So he commanded his army to follow the Israelites, capture them, and bring them back.

When the Israelites reached the Red Sea and saw Pharaoh's armies coming, they thought they would be caught because the water was too deep to cross. But God had another plan. God told Moses that he would help the Israelites. All Moses had to do was stretch out his staff, and the water would part. Exactly how this happened is still a mystery, but God created a dry path in the middle of the sea, on which the Israelites could cross. Just as the last Israelite made it safely to the other side of the sea, the Egyptian army started to cross, but when they got half way the water came back together and covered the Egyptian soldiers. (Exodus 12:33-51 & 14:1-31)

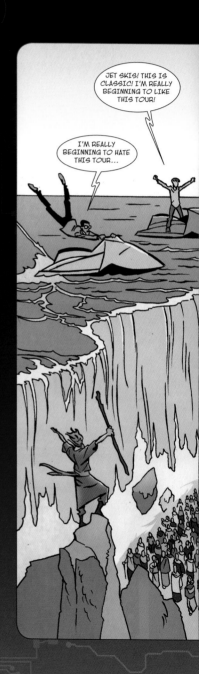

at sinai

Since leaving Egypt, God's people had witnessed the ten plagues, been released from slavery, saw the Red Sea part, and the Egyptian Army stopped. You would think they would be happy. But it wasn't long after they left Egypt that some of the people started to grumble and complain. Even though God had provided all the water they needed and a special type of food called Manna, which could be found on the ground each morning, the people still complained. Some of the Israelites even wanted to go back to Egypt and become slaves again rather than trust God.

For three months, the Israelites walked through the wilderness until they came to a mountain called Sinai. This was the same area where God had spoken to Moses through the burning bush.

When the Israelites arrived at Mount Sinai, they pitched their tents at the base of the mountain while Moses went up to the top of the mountain to speak with God. While there, God gave Moses the Ten Commandments that were carved on two stones. These Ten Commandments described how God expected the Israelites to live. (Exodus 19 & 20)

42

THE TEN COMMANDMENTS

The Ten Commandments were given to Moses while he was at the top of Mount Sinai. God not only told Moses what the Ten Commandments were, but he carved them into two stone tablets with his finger. These Ten Commandments were to be the basic rules by which the people of Israel would live their lives. The first four commandments describe how the people of Israel were to live in relationship with God, while the last six commandments describe how the people were to live in relationship with each other.

THE GOLDEN CALF

While Moses was up on the top of Mount Sinai getting the Ten Commandments from God, the people began to wonder what had happened to him because he had been gone for such a long time. Fearing that Moses was not coming back, the people asked Aaron, Moses' brother, to make an idol out of the gold they had brought from Egypt. Aaron formed the gold into the shape of a calf, which the people danced around and worshipped as their god.

When Moses came down from the top of the mountain and saw the people and saw what the people were doing with the golden calf, he became very angry. He threw down the tablets on which the Ten Commandments were written, and they broke into pieces. Moses then had the golden calf destroyed. (Exodus 32)

THE TEN COMMANDMENTS FOR YOUNG PEOPLE

1) You may not love anyone or anything more than you love God (including money or computer games).

2) Worship only God. Do not worship (or consider more important) any person or thing above God—not your parents, friends, celebrities, athletes—not a cat or boat or skateboard—nothing!

3) Do not swear. Use God's holy name only in a loving way, never to express anger or frustration. (A wise person once said: If a person cusses a lot, he or she isn't witty enough to think of something better to say.)

4) Work only six days a week. Set aside one day for rest, worshiping of God, and meeting with other Christians.

5) Respect your parents. Love them, and the Lord will reward you with long life.

6) You may not hate other people; don't plan how to hurt someone, and definitely don't murder!

7) Keep your thoughts and actions in check. Be self-controlled. Remember, your body is a temple of God.

8) Don't steal.

9) Don't lie. Lying leads to more lies, and you have to remember what you said about something and to whom, and it makes everything complicated and stressful. Lies hurt people and can destroy relationships. Just be honest!

10) Don't be jealous of other people's stuff. Don't envy your friend's electronic games, clothes, big house, car, or anything. Be thankful for what you have.

In addition to the Ten Commandments, God also gave Moses instructions on how to construct a building where the Israelites could come and worship him. The place of worship was to be called a tabernacle. The word

tabernacle means tent, or a place where people dwell. In the Bible it symbolized the place where God's people could come and fellowship with him. The Tabernacle was a portable building that the Israelites could take apart and move as needed—which would come in handy during their forty years of wandering in the desert. The Tabernacle was an area enclosed by a tall wall. Inside stood an altar, a laver (or a place to wash), and a large tent. The tent was very special and was called the Tent of Meeting because it was here that God met with the priests, who were from the tribe of Levi.

Moses had several pieces of furniture built to go inside the tabernacle area (Genesis 25-27). One of the more important pieces of furniture was the ark of the covenant that was located inside the Tent of Meeting. The ark God had Moses build was not a boat, like in Genesis 6, but was a large box covered in gold. It was about two feet wide, four feet long, and two feet high. Two cherubim angels were placed on top of the ark facing each other with their wings stretched upward. Finally, there were two golden rings on each side of the ark. The people made two long poles that slid through the rings on each side in order to carry the ark from place to place. The poles were used because God has said that no one was allowed to touch the ark. God also commanded the people to put three items inside the ark to remember how he had provided for them in the past. The three items were the two tablets containing the Ten Commandments, a golden jar of manna, and Aaron's staff that had sprouted leaves. (Hebrews 9:4)

WORSHIP IN THE TABERNACLE

Although all of the Israelites worshiped God at the tabernacle, only the priests were allowed to enter the special room called the Holy of Holies. Everyday, sacrifices were offered on an altar in the courtyard that surrounded the Tent of Meeting.

The Tent of Meeting was divided into two rooms, the Holy Place and the Most Holy Place, also called the "Holy of Holies." It was in the Holy of Holies that the Ark of the Covenant was held. Only the high priest was allowed to enter into the Holy of Holies, and this happened only once a year on the Day of Atonement.

This structure of the tabernacle was used until King Solomon built the Temple, which was based on the same layout as the Tabernacle.

THE LAW - LEVITICUS

The book of Leviticus talks about the laws God gave to Moses for the people of Israel. "Leviticus" means "about the Levites." God made the tribe of Levi responsible for everything related to worshipping God and the laws of God.

God told the Israelites how they should live with each other, how they should treat each other, and how they should worship God. The law also told the Israelites how to bring sacrifices to God, what they shouldn't eat, and lots of other rules to use in their daily routines and to live together as a nation. In addition to the Ten Commandments, according to Jewish tradition, God gave Moses 613 laws. That's a lot to remember!

But God's laws were not because God wanted to make life difficult. God's laws actually helped his people stay healthy and live together peacefully. He also wanted his people to be different from the other nations that lived around them. (Exodus 21-23)

NUMBERS

The book of Numbers records the forty years of Israel's wandering in the desert and of the counting of the people. When a government or king wanted to know how many people lived in a certain area, they would take a census. Countries still take a census today to find out how many people live in their land.

Counting how many people made up each of the twelve tribes of Israel helped Moses to divide up land and know how many men could join the army.

Many ancient kings took a census of their people to see how much money they could collect in taxes.

OH NO! MY RSP IS MISSING. I DROPPED IT SOMEWHERE. HELP ME FIND IT! I DON'T WANT TO GET STUCK HERE!

EVERYBODY LOOK. WE'VE GOT TO FIND THAT THING.

THE TWELVE TRIBES

Jacob had twelve sons, and their descendants became the twelve tribes of Israel. They were called the tribes of Israel because Jacob's name was changed to "Israel" when he was older. The twelve original tribes were:

Reuben	Judah
Zebulun	Dan
Gad	Ephraim
Simeon	Issachar
Benjamin	Asher
Naphtali	Manasseh

But what about Joseph, the most famous son of Jacob? Two of the tribes, Ephraim and Manasseh, were named after Joseph's two sons.

That means another son was not named. Can you guess which one? The answer is mentioned in the section about the tabernacle. It was Levi. Because the Levities were the priests of God, they were not given a section of land. Instead, they were scattered among the other tribes, and their job was to help the Israelites in their worship of God.

THE TWELVE SPIES & CANAAN

After traveling from Egypt and experiencing some remarkable events at Sinai, the Israelites finally arrived at the edge of the land of Canaan. Canaan was the land that God promised to give to Abraham back in Genesis. Before going in, however, Moses and several other leaders decided to send twelve spies into the land to look around.

The spies were gone for forty days before they returned with a report about what they had seen. They told the leaders that the land had plenty of resources to take care of the Israelites, another way of saying it was a land flowing with "milk and honey." However, there was a problem. The people living in the land were really, really big. Ten of the spies didn't want to enter the land because they were afraid of the people living there. Joshua and Caleb were the only two spies who wanted to attack. They remembered God's promise and believed he would help them take possession of Canaan.

Unfortunately, the leaders ignored Joshua and Caleb. The leaders let their fear get the better of them and didn't trust in God, even though he had brought them out of Egypt, showed them miracle after miracle, and provided for them the whole time.

God was very angry and decided that those who did not trust him would never enter the Promised Land. God told the Israelites that the whole nation would wander through the desert for forty years. Only those under the age of twenty-one would be allowed to enter into the Promised Land, but God allowed Joshua and Caleb into Canaan, since they had believed in him.

FORTY YEARS IN THE WILDERNESS

People who did not trust that God would deliver them into the Promised Land were punished for their lack of faith. God made them wander in the wilderness for forty years. During those forty years, the Israelites met some of the new neighbors, but the neighborhood wasn't very friendly. They had trouble with the Edomites, the Amorites, and several other small nations around Canaan.

The Israelites turned out to be good fighters, and with the Lord's help they defeated several of the small nations that tried to keep Israel away from Canaan. One king, Balak of Moab, was afraid of these new people and asked a man named Balaam to put a curse on Israel. As Balaam traveled to meet with the king of Moab, God spoke to him and said, "You must not put a curse on those people, because they are blessed." (Numbers 22:12) Balaam told his guides to leave because he was not going to curse this group of people. The king of Moab was insistent that Balaam curse the Israelites, and after many refusals, Balaam performed his ceremony. But in the end, God put the words in Balaam's mouth, and Balaam blessed the Israelites instead of cursing them.

Fun Fact: The Edomites were descendants of Esau. The Moabites and Ammonites were descendants of Lot (Abraham's nephew).

⊗

ADVENTURE READINGS

Adventure Reading: While on his journey, Balaam was outsmarted by his donkey. The donkey saved Balaam's life. (Numbers 22:21-41)

ACTUALLY, THEY'RE DECIDING WHETHER TO TAKE OVER THE PROMISED LAND. THEIR SPIES SCOUTED AHEAD AND THINK IT MIGHT NOT BE EASY TO CONQUER.

MAYBE THEY SHOULD FLIP A COIN.

OR DO ROCK, PAPER, SCISSORS.

GETTING READY TO CONQUER CANAAN

After wandering in the desert for forty years, the people of Israel were finally ready to enter the Promised Land. Before entering, Moses went over the laws that God gave in Exodus 20 so the people would know what was expected of them as they entered a new chapter in their lives. The book of Deuteronomy records what Moses said. He reminded Israel how God wanted them to act and live together, and how they should treat the strangers they would meet in the new land. God wanted the Israelites to remove everyone who already lived in Canaan so the people of Israel wouldn't be tempted by the evil beliefs and actions of the Canaanites.

Moses went with the Israelites to Canaan, but he couldn't enter the land himself. Joshua (one of the spies who had trusted God) took over as leader. Under Joshua's command, the Israelites entered the Promised Land after wandering in the desert for forty years.

THE PROMISED LAND

Canaan was the area of land God gave to Abraham that was renamed the Promised Land. Following the forty years of wandering, the Israelites who entered the land began to conquer city after city and claim the land as their own.

Across the Jordan River, in the land of Canaan, the city of Jericho was the first obstacle to Israel taking possession of the Promised Land. Like many years earlier, spies were sent ahead to check out the city. The spies discovered that Jericho was surrounded by a very tall wall used to protect the people from invading armies. While they were in Jericho, a woman named Rahab hid the spies from the city guards. In return, Rahab was saved from the city's destruction.

JOSHUA CAPTURES JERICHO

The Israelites captured the city of Jericho in a unique way. Instead of attacking the city, as most armies would have done, Israel was instructed by God to simply walk around the city, silently, once a day for six days. On the seventh day, the people and the priests were to walk around the city seven times. On the seventh time around the priests were to blow trumpets, and the people were to yell as loud as they could. As Israel did as God said, the earth began to shake, and the walls of Jericho came tumbling down. The city had been captured, even with its massive walls for protection.

News spread quickly to the other nations around about how Israel had captured the great city of Jericho. God was on Israel's side, and as long as they believed and trusted him, they continued to conquer other cities in Canaan.

Eventually the land was divided among the twelve tribes of Israel. Unfortunately the people did not remove all of the inhabitants in the land as God had commanded. As a result, Israel never experienced lasting peace and never possessed all of the land God had promised to Abraham. (Joshua 2:1-24; 3:1-17; 6:1-27)

THE CANAANITES

The Canaanites had many gods, but the most important ones were Baal, Astarte, and Dagon. The worship of these gods often involved practices the Israelites knew were evil—even human sacrifices.

The Canaanites lived in cities, each with its own king. To us, the Canaanite cities wouldn't seem large, but the city walls were enormous—up to ten feet thick.

Hazor, the largest city in Canaan, was less than a quarter of a square mile in size, but it was surrounded by walls that were 100 feet thick!

THE JUDGES

After the people of Israel had been living in the Promised Land for many years, there came a time when they forgot the teachings of Moses and the miracles that God had done. The people also forgot their promise to obey God's laws and live according to his commandments.

Following the death of Joshua, each tribe established its own leader to govern the piece of land they had been given. When the people turned their attention away from God and began to live however they wanted, God stopped protecting them. As time went on, the surrounding nations began to attack and overthrow certain parts of the Promised Land. This happened several times. And each time, the people would eventually realize they had done wrong, and return to God, and ask for forgiveness. In response, God gave the Israelites special leaders called judges to help them out of their situation. These individuals, or judges, led the people in both military and civil matters. In all, there were thirteen judges who ruled over a four hundred year period. The names of the thirteen judges were Othniel, Ehud, Shamgar, Deborah, Barak, Gideon, Tola, Jair, Jephthah, Ibzan, Elon, Abdon, and Samson. (Judges 1-21)

EHUD

During one of the times of Israel's disobedience, God allowed Eglon, King of the Moabites, to attack and conquer the people. Eglon was very fat and made the people that his armies conquered pay high taxes to him. The king threatened to kill all the people of the captured land if the taxes weren't paid. This is when God called Ehud to be a judge and help deliver the people of Israel from Eglon.

When the time came for the tax to be brought to King Eglon, Ehud decided to go himself. As was the normal practice, when Ehud arrived he was searched by the king's guards. Because the guards did not find any weapons on Ehud, they allowed him to go in and give the tax money to King Eglon. Once the money was paid, Ehud told the king that he had a secret message from God. King Eglon had the room cleared, and Ehud was allowed to approach the king. Once Ehud was close enough, he stabbed the king with a short sword that he had hidden. Ehud then left the room through another door and locked it behind him. After a while the king's servants became worried and had the door opened and found that the king was dead. In all the confusion, Ehud escaped.

After that, Ehud led the Israelites in battle against the Moabites, and since God was with them, the Israelite people gained their freedom and lived in peace for about eighty years. (Judges 3:12-30)

THE ISRAELITES HAVE A LOT OF BATTLES TO FIGHT.

IT'S A GOOD THING THEY HAVE GOD ON THEIR SIDE!

Deborah became a judge of Israel after Ehud's death. She would meet with the people of Israel to review their disputes under a palm tree between Ramah and Bethel. One day Deborah received a word from God that Barak should take ten thousand men and go fight against King Jabin, who was oppressing the Israelites. Barak asked that Deborah accompany him on this mission, and she agreed to go. Barak's army was successful and defeated King Jabin's army. To celebrate, Deborah and Barak sang a song about how God won the battle for Israel.

(Judges 4 & 5)

GIDEON

Gideon was the sixth judge God raised up to deliver Israel from their troubles. When he became judge, the Israelites were being oppressed by the Midianites. One day, while Gideon did his chores, the angel of the Lord appeared and told Gideon that the Lord wanted him to lead Israel and defeat the Midianites. Gideon built an alter called "The Lord is Peace," gave thanks, and made an offering.

The Lord told Gideon to pull down the altar of Baal and the Asherah pole that was in his yard, and Gideon did as he was told. But Gideon wasn't sure he was the one to be a leader for Israel. So Gideon asked for a sign from God. Gideon put a blanket made from sheepskin on the ground and asked God to let the sheepskin be wet with dew in the morning, but not the ground around it. The next morning the fleece was exactly as Gideon had asked, the dew was only on the blanket but not on the ground.

Still, Gideon asked for another sign, just to be sure. This time he asked for the opposite, that the dew be on the ground but not on the fleece sheepskin. The next morning, the ground was wet with dew but the fleece was dry.

Being confident of God's call on his life, Gideon gathered together an army to battle against the Midianites. Gideon started out with 32,000 soldiers, but God said it was too many. Twice God sent some of the men away, until only 300 were left to battle the Midianites. Each man had a clay pitcher in one hand and a trumpet in the other. When the three hundred men approached the Midianite camp, they blew their trumpets and smashed the pitchers. The Midianites became confused and thought they were surrounded by a large army. They ran into each other and began killing each other! Those left alive ran away. After this, Gideon was asked to become king, but he declined and declared that the "Lord shall rule over you." And the Israelite people lived in peace for many years. (Judges 6:11-8:35)

SAMSON

Samson was the last judge who God called to protect Israel. He was best known for his incredible strength and long hair, and he fought many battles against the Philistines. In fact, in one battle alone, Samson killed one thousand soldiers with only the jawbone of a donkey as his weapon. (Judges 15:15)

During his lifetime, the Israelites began to marry people from other nations, which God had told them not to do. Even Samson fell in love with a very beautiful Philistine woman named Delilah. When the Philistine leaders heard about this, they asked Delilah to act as a spy. They wanted her to find out why Samson was so strong. Samson revealed to Delilah that if his hair was cut, he would lose his strength. Soon Samson fell asleep and Delilah cut his hair. When Samson awoke he realized what had happened. Because his strength was gone, he was captured, blinded, and thrown into prison by the Philistines.

Years later, at a celebration, Samson was led out of the prison to be laughed at by the Philistines. The guards placed Samson between two pillars that supported the building where the party was being held. The leaders had never considered that Samson's strength might return. As Samson stood between the pillars, he asked God for forgiveness and to return his strength one last time. God answered his prayer. Samson pushed the pillars apart until the roof crashed down. (Judges 14-16)

RUTH & BOAZ

Though the Israelites had been given the land of Canaan by God, during the days of the judges, some families decided to move in with other nations. Elimelech and his family, originally from Bethlehem, decided to move to Moab.

Remember, when the Israelites first arrived in the Promised Land, God commanded them not to marry anyone from another nation. This command was given because the other nations worshiped idols and did not believe in God. When it came time for Elimelech's sons to get married, they disobeyed God's command, and each married a woman from Moab.

Years passed, and Elimelech and his sons died, leaving Elimelech's wife Naomi alone with her two daughters-in-law, Ruth and Orpah. Naomi decided to move back to Bethlehem to the area where her relatives lived. She told Ruth and Orpah to stay in their own homeland. Orpah decided to stay, but Ruth loved Naomi and went with her to Bethlehem.

In Bethlehem, Ruth met Boaz, a rich farmer who followed God's law and provided for the needy in his community. Boaz and Ruth fell in love and got married. One of their descendants was King David, the greatest King of Israel. Another descendant, who would be born more than a thousand years later, was Jesus Christ. (Ruth 1-4)

Fun Fact: In Bible times, if a man died without having any children, his widow had to marry his closest relative (his brother or cousin). Then when the widow had children, they would be considered the children of the man who had died and they could inherit his land. This relative who married the widow was called the "kinsman-redeemer."

Samuel

Hannah was a young woman who served the Lord faithfully, but she was not able to have a child. She prayed daily for a child and went to the tabernacle each year to worship God. One year, while she was worshipping at the tabernacle, she cried out to God, asking for a son and promising that if he would give her one, she would dedicate his life to God's service. God heard her prayer, and the next year Hannah became pregnant and gave birth to a baby boy. She named him Samuel, which means "asked of God."

When Samuel was about three years old, Hannah took him, as promised, to the tabernacle to be trained in God's laws. From that time on, Samuel lived at the tabernacle with a priest named Eli.

Several years later, Samuel was woken up in the middle of the night by a voice calling his name. He got up and went to Eli to see if he had called him, but Eli said it wasn't him and to go back to bed. So Samuel went back to his bed and fell asleep. A few minutes later he heard the voice calling his name again and rushed into Eli's room to see what he wanted. Again Eli said it wasn't him. When this happened a third time, Eli realized that it was God calling Samuel's name and told the young man that the next time he heard the voice to say, "Speak, for your servant is listening." God did call Samuel again and Samuel responded as Eli had instructed him. Samuel served many years in God's service and became a great teacher and prophet. He was the last of the judges. (1 Samuel & 2 Samuel)

GOD SHOWS HIS POWER TO THE PHILISTINES

The Philistines lived along the edge of the Mediterranean Sea and were known for their ability to sail and fish. They were also a constant problem for the people of Israel.

On one occasion, the Israelites went to battle, and they took the Ark of the Covenant out of the Tabernacle and placed it in front of their army. They trusted the ark, not God. The result was God let the Philistines defeat the Israelites, capture the ark, and place it in the temple of their god, Dagon.

The next morning, however, when the priests came into the temple, they witnessed a disturbing sight. The statue of Dagon was found lying on the ground in front of the ark. The priests wondered how this could have happened since no one had been in the room since the ark was placed there the night before. So the priests set the statue back up and went about their business. The following morning the priests again found the statue on the ground, but this time its head and hands had been broken off. After this, many bad things began to happen to the Philistines, so they decided to send the ark back to the Israelites where it belonged.

YEAH. OTHER BAD THINGS HAPPENED TO THEM AS WELL. THEY DECIDED TO RETURN THE ARK TO THE ISRAELITES.

THAT MUST HAVE BEEN SO EMBARRASSING FOR THE PHILISTINES.

I HOPE THEY HAD THEIR RECEIPT! YOU CAN'T RETURN ANYTHING WITHOUT A RECEIPT.

THEY DIDN'T BUY THE ARK, YOU GOOFBALL; THEY CAPTURED IT IN BATTLE.

OH. THAT'S DIFFERENT THEN.

IT'S LIKE DAGON IS BOWING DOWN TO THE LORD!

SAUL, THE FIRST KING

The Israelites decided that they wanted a king so they could be like the rest of the nations surrounding them. So the leaders of the people went to Samuel and asked him to appoint a king to rule over them. The Israelites did not care that God was their King and had taken care of them for many years. What the people wanted was a physical king whom they could see and talk with.

Saul was the man chosen by God to be the Israel's first king. During his rule, Saul led Israel to victory against the Ammonites and many other nations. At first, Saul was like most other kings, but as he became older he began turning away from God and made decisions without God's instruction. In time, God told Samuel to tell Saul that he was going to replace him with another king; a king who would listen and follow God's laws. (1 Samuel 8:1-22)

Fun Fact: In most societies around Israel, the king was considered to be a god.

DAVID IS CHOSEN

David was the youngest son of Jesse. He worked as a shepherd taking care of the flocks. One day, Samuel came to Jesse's house to see his sons in order to pick the next King of Israel. All of Jesse's sons lined up before Samuel, except David, who was still in the fields with the sheep. Because David was the youngest, and the smallest, he was not invited. Nobody thought he could possibly be named king. Samuel looked at each son, but God did not choose any of them. Finally, Samuel asked Jesse, "Are these all of your children?" Jesse replied, "There remains yet the youngest, and behold he is tending the sheep." Samuel requested that David be brought to him. When David came to the house, God told Samuel, "Arise, anoint him; for this is he." Samuel did as he was commanded and anointed David to become the next King of Israel. (1 Samuel 16)

WHAT IS "ANOINTING"?

"Anointing" in the act by which oil is rubbed, smeared, or poured on something, or someone. It was a sacred act in the Old Testament that symbolized the choosing of someone for a special work. For example, David was anointed by Samuel to serve as Israel's next king. When Samuel placed the oil on David in front of his family, it signified that David had been set aside for a special purpose.

EVERYONE WATCH CLOSELY. THIS IS A SPECIAL MOMENT IN THE BIBLE. IT'S WHEN DAVID GETS GOD'S ANOINTMENT TO BE KING OF ISRAEL.

WHY DOES HE NEED OINTMENT? DID HE BUMP HIS HEAD?

GOD'S OINTMENT? MUST BE POWERFUL STUFF.

MAYBE HE HAS A FEVER.

OR A HEADACHE.

WHEN I BUMP MY HEAD, MOM JUST GIVES ME A BAND-AID.

NO, NO! SAMUEL'S PUTTING OIL ON HIS HEAD, NOT OINTMENT. DAVID IS BEING ANOINTED! IT'S A VERY IMPORTANT ACT WHICH SHOWS THAT GOD HAS CHOSEN DAVID TO SERVE HIM IN A SPECIAL WAY.

DAVID AND GOLIATH

During one of Israel's battles against the Philistines, a challenge was given that instead of both armies fighting each other, which would only end in many people dying, each army would send out their best fighter. Whichever warrior won the fight, the other nation would surrender as if the whole army had been defeated.

The Philistines chose a fighter named Goliath. He was about nine feet tall and very strong. Because of his size, none of the Israelites wanted to fight him. It happened at the same time that David had come to visit his brothers and heard about the challenge. Because he knew God was on Israel's side, he volunteered to fight Goliath. Many laughed at David because he was so small, but no one volunteered to fight in his place.

David went onto the battlefield and faced Goliath, who was angry because it seemed that Israel had sent a boy to fight him. David took out his slingshot and placed a smooth stone in it. Being a shepherd, David had learned to use a slingshot very well. David was also confident that God would protect him.

David began to sling the stone above his head then let it go. The stone hit Goliath on his forehead and he fell down unconscious. David took Goliath's sword and killed him.

Instantly, David became a hero in Israel and King Saul gave him a position in his army. (1 Samuel 17:1–58)

The more popular David became, the more jealous and angry Saul got. Finally, it got so bad that Saul wanted to kill David, and David had to hide in caves in the wilderness of Judah.

Even while David was running for his life from Saul, David's best friend was Saul's son, Jonathan. David and Jonathan's friendship was one of the most famous friendships in the Bible. (1 Samuel 20:1-42)

Still, David didn't understand why God made him suffer and be hunted like an animal, even though God had told David that he would be king. David cried out to God, and many of his prayers make up the book of Psalms. One question David asked is why do bad things happen to good people? Another person in the Bible asked that same question—Job. The book of Job was written so long ago, that David may actually have read it—and David could definitely relate to Job's suffering.

THE LIFE OF JOB

Job was a rich man who owned 7,000 sheep, 3,000 camels, 500 oxen, 500 donkeys, lots of land and many servants. He also had seven sons and three daughters and was a faithful man of God. One day, Satan requested that God remove the protection he had around Job to see if Job would remain faithful to God even if everything he had were taken away.

God agreed, and Job lost everything. He lost his sheep, camels, oxen, donkeys, land, servants, and even his children. To make things worse, Job also lost his health, and painful sores appeared all over his body. Job did not understand why all these bad things were happening to him, but he continued to trust God.

Hearing of his troubles, Job's friends, Eliphaz, Bildad, and Zophar, came for a visit. They told Job that he must have done something wrong to have all these bad things happen. But Job knew in his heart that he had not done anything wrong. Even though Job questioned God about his situation, he never rejected or turned away from God. He continued to trust God, and God rewarded Job. God vindicated Job to his friends and let them know they were wrong about Job, and he hadn't sinned. God gave Job back his health and wealth and even gave him more children. Job was faithful to God through the bad times and the good, just as David was faithful to God when the road was rough. (Job 1-42)

DAVID AS KING

After Saul's death, David became king. He captured the city of Jebus, which was in the center of his Kingdom. Back then, the city was still small but very difficult to capture because it was built on a rock that stuck out from the hillside, with valleys on three sides.

David's soldiers entered the city by crawling up through a water shaft that went down from the city into the valley. David made Jebus his capital and renamed it Jerusalem, which means "city of peace."

David wanted to build a temple for God in Jerusalem, but he was not allowed to do this during his reign as king. He did, however, bring the Ark of the Covenant back to Jerusalem. As the ark was led through the city, there was a great celebration and David danced.

JERUSALEM AND DAVID

• David was 37 when he conquered the city of Jerusalem.

• Jerusalem is about 3,800 years old—much older than the Bible's first mention of it.

• Three of the world's largest religions—Judaism, Christianity, and Islam—all consider Jerusalem to be a holy city.

ADVENTURE READINGS ⊗

David was a good ruler, loved music, and was a writer. In fact, David wrote many of the Psalms. (2 Samuel 5:1-12 , 6:1-23 and 7:11b-16)

Even though David was a man of God and had God's favor upon him, David was not a perfect man. Israel also still had many enemies like the Philistines, Ammonites and Edomites. Fighting was a common occurrence in the region, but with God's help, David's armies continued to win the battles. David was a good king who provided for and protected his people.

One day, David didn't go out to fight at the head of his army as usual. David stayed home to rest. That evening David took a walk out onto his rooftop. While on the roof, David spotted a beautiful young woman named Bathsheba on another roof below. David became infatuated with this woman and wanted her to become his new wife. However, there was a problem because Bathsheba was already married to a soldier in the army named Uriah.

David began to scheme how he could get Bathsheba to become his wife and came up with the plan to put Uriah at the front of the army where he would have a good chance of being killed in a battle. David's plan worked and Uriah was killed. David had Bathsheba brought to the palace to become his wife.

Even though David had always been a good man, he did make a horrible mistake and allowed his judgment to become tainted by sin. David knew it was wrong to covet another man's wife but this did not stop him from making poor choices. God became angry with David and sent a prophet named Nathan to confront him.

David was sorry for his actions and asked God for forgiveness. God did forgive him, but because David sinned, there were still consequences. One of those consequences was that David's household and kingdom would always be in turmoil and would be people fighting against one another.

DAVID & ABSALOM:

One way David's family turned against one another was through his son, Absalom. Absalom was actually born to Bathsheba, so Absalom was actually born as a result of David's sin.

One day Absalom decided he wanted to be king and started plotting against his father. Absalom even gathered together an army to fight his father. This betrayal broke David's heart but David did fight him for the sake of his kingdom. In the end, Absalom had to run for his life. While trying to escape, the mule he was riding ran under a tree, but Absalom did not duck, and his long hair became tangled in the tree's branches. David's army commander found Absalom hanging from the tree by his hair and killed him for treason. Absalom was killed for treason because of his actions but this did not stop.

THE PSALMS

The book of Psalms is actually a book of songs—one hundred and fifty to be exact. Many of the psalms were set to music and were used in Israel's worship of God. You might think of the book of Psalms as a collection of worship songs used by Israel during the Old Testament times, and many are still used in worship songs today.

The Psalms are basically prayers that cover an intense range of emotions, from sadness and despair to joy and praise. Some even express anger at God! If a person felt guilty because of something they did, they could use a psalm to confess their sins to God. David wrote many of the psalms. In Psalm 51, David cries to God and asks for mercy and forgiveness for his sins. Despite his sins, God forgave David because David was sincere. God searched David's heart and knew he was truly repentant, sorry for what he had done. And God blessed David with another son, Solomon, who became the next king.

WE HAVE SOME TIME BEFORE WE REACH OUR NEXT STOP. SO WHY DON'T WE ALL SING A PRAISE SONG TO GOD AS WE TRAVEL! THAT'LL HELP YOU GUYS UNDERSTAND WHAT THE BOOK OF PSALMS IS ALL ABOUT.

WE'VE MADE UP SOME MUSIC TO GO WITH ONE OF THE PSALMS. OPEN THE BIBLES WE PASSED OUT TO PSALM 150. JOSH AND I WILL START SINGING THE WORDS, AND YOU CAN JUMP IN AS SOON AS YOU LEARN THE MELODY.

OH, MAN. I CAN'T SING.

REMEMBER WHEN YOU WISHED YOU WERE BOLD ENOUGH TO DO THINGS WITHOUT WORRYING ABOUT WHAT OTHER PEOPLE THINK? NOW'S YOUR CHANCE!

adventure readings

**Sing to the Lord a new song;
sing to the Lord, all the earth.**

Psalm 96:1-3   Psalm 23

Psalm 37   Psalm 100

Psalm 32   Psalm 130

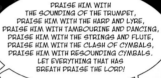

SOLOMON

David had many sons and daughters, but it was his son Solomon who became King of Israel after him. David advised his son to always remember to keep God's laws. After Solomon became king, God gave Solomon great wisdom with which to rule the people of Israel. Solomon remembered the favor that God bestowed upon his father. He prayed and asked God to give him wisdom, understanding, and a discerning heart, so he could be a good king. God was pleased. Solomon could have asked for riches or power, but he asked for wisdom instead, so God granted Solomon's request and also gave him those things he did not ask for—riches, honor, and power. God said, "I have given you a wise and discerning heart, so that there has been no one like you before you, nor shall one like you arise after you." **(1 Kings 3:12, NASB)**

One example of Solomon's great wisdom was demonstrated in a dispute between two women who each claimed that a certain baby was theirs. As king, Solomon allowed both women to tell their side of the story as to why the baby was hers. He then decreed that the baby was to be cut in half and that each woman was to be given half of the baby. One of the women thought this would be a good idea, but the other woman thought this was a horrible decision and asked that the baby be given to the other woman. Solomon knew that the true mother would not want the baby to die.

Later in Solomon's life, he fulfilled his father's desire by building a temple for God. It took over seven years and approximately 30,000 men to build the temple. This became the place where Israel would come to worship God. Inside, like the tabernacle, there was the Holy Place and the Most Holy Place, where the Ark of the Covenant was placed. The temple stood for about five hundred years, until it was destroyed by King Nebuchadnezzar.

AND NOW HERE WE ARE, IN KING SOLOMON'S DAY.

FOR A LONG TIME THE ISRAELITES WORSHIPED GOD AT THE TABERNACLE—A TEMPORARY, PORTABLE TENT.

NOW, AT LAST, GOD HAD GIVEN THEM AN ACTUAL BUILDING WHERE THEY COULD WORSHIP HIM. A PLACE TRULY FIT FOR THAT PURPOSE!

SOLOMON DID MORE THAN BUILD THE TEMPLE. GOD GAVE HIM LOTS OF WISDOM.

SO HE WROTE MANY PROVERBS, WHICH ARE WISE SAYINGS ABOUT HOW TO LIVE WELL.

PROVERBS

King Solomon searched for wisdom, praying to live as God would want in all situations, and he recorded what he learned. Solomon wrote many tidbits of advice on living in the book of Proverbs. In fact, Solomon wrote most of the book of Proverbs. A proverb is a short saying, or truism, about life, usually written metaphorically, like, "The wise in heart are called discerning, and gracious words promote instruction." (Proverbs 16:21) "Many call Proverbs the book of wisdom because it contains truths that help people live life in a wise way.

"Trust in the Lord with all your heart and lean not on your own understanding; in all your ways submit to him, and he will make your paths straight." Proverbs 3:5-6

"A generous person will prosper; whoever refreshes others will be refreshed." Proverbs 11:25

"Whoever fears the Lord has a secure fortress, and for their children it will be a refuge." Proverbs 14:26

"A Gentle answer turns away wrath, but a harsh word stirs up anger." Proverbs 15:1

"Whoever gives heed to instruction prospers, and blessed is the one who trusts in the Lord." Proverbs 16:20

"Train a child in the way he should go, and when he is old he will not turn from it." Proverbs 22:6

SOLOMON'S RICHES

Under King Solomon's rule, Israel was a prosperous, peaceful country. Solomon was so famous that many rulers around the world wanted to meet Solomon. One of those people was the queen of Sheba. She left her country in southern Arabia, some 1,200 miles from Jerusalem and took the long camel ride across the hot desert. The queen of Sheba brought with her many treasures including various spices. In the days of Solomon, spices were a valuable commodity. The cinnamon that was presented at court was truly a royal gift. The queen was very impressed with King Solomon and his kingdom. She even praised the God of Israel for what he had done for his people.

GOLD...

SILVER...

IVORY...

REMEMBER WHEN I SAID THAT KING SOLOMON WAS RICH? TAKE A LOOK AT SOME OF THE COOL STUFF HE HAD.

HOW RICH WAS SOLOMON?

To get an idea of Solomon's riches, read 1 Kings 10:14-29. You'll see that one of the things he received was gold—666 talents every year. That's about 22,000 kilograms of gold. Today that would be enough money to buy a ten-dollar pizza for every man, woman, and child in Alaska, Arizona, Colorado, Idaho, Montana, Nebraska, Nevada, New Mexico, North Dakota, Oregon, South Dakota, Utah, Washington, and Wyoming—with enough money left over for a big tip for the totally exhausted delivery person.

ECCLESIASTES

The phrase, "Vanity, vanity, everything is vanity," is one of the most famous quotes from King Solomon. Another way of say this is "Meaningless! Meaningless! Everything is meaningless!" When you read through the book of Ecclesiastes, you discover that this saying does not mean that everything in the world is worthless, but that without a correct relationship with God, the things we do in this life have no purpose. However, when we know God, we can enjoy the things he has created and use them in our lives correctly.

Ultimately, the book of Ecclesiastes gives information about various experiences in life and the importance of being faithful to God no matter what. (Ecclesiastes 1:1-14 and Ecclesiastes 12:1, 9-14)

"For everything there is a season, and a time for every matter under heaven:

A time to be born, and a time to die;

A time to plant, and a time to pluck up what is planted;

A time to kill, and a time to heal;

A time to break down, and a time to build up;

A time to weep, and a time to laugh;

A time to mourn, and a time to dance;

A time to cast away stones, and a time to gather stones together;

A time to embrace, and a time to refrain from embracing;

A time to seek, and a time to lose;

A time to keep, and a time to cast away;

A time to tear, and a time to sew;

A time to keep silence, and a time to speak;

A time to love, and a time to hate;

A time for war, and a time for peace."

Ecclesiastes 3:1-8, ESV

87

SONG OF SONGS

The Song of Solomon, or what is sometimes called the Song of Songs, is a poem about love. Why include a poem about love in the Bible? The Song of Solomon shows that there is a special bond of love between a man and a woman, and that God wants us to know about this amazing relationship.

In chapter four of Song of Songs, Solomon described his love for a woman. He told her about how beautiful she was to him, but the terms he used to illustrate her beauty seem somewhat crazy to us today.

"… Her eyes are like doves"

TOBY'S RIGHT! DOESN'T THE BIBLE SAY, "SEEK AND YOU WILL FIND"?

YES, IT DOES. THOSE WERE JESUS' WORDS. BUT HE WASN'T TALKING ABOUT FINDING YOUR EARTHLY FATHER...

YOU KNOW, KIDS, I'M SURE GOD WANTED YOU TO JOIN OUR TOUR SO YOU COULD FIND YOUR DAD. BUT MAYBE HE HAD SOMETHING EVEN MORE IMPORTANT IN MIND. MAYBE GOD WANTED YOU TO FIND YOUR HEAVENLY FATHER!

WOW!

DOUBLE WOW!

"… Your neck is like the tower of David built with rows of stones, on which are hung a thousand shields."

"… Her hair [was] like a flock of goats."

YOUR HEAVENLY FATHER LOVES YOU AND WANTS TO BE WITH YOU AND HAVE A CLOSE RELATIONSHIP WITH YOU. SO WHILE MICK AND I HELP YOU FIND YOUR DAD, HOW ABOUT IF WE ALSO HELP YOU FIND GOD?

SPEAKING OF LOVE, THERE ARE ALL KINDS OF LOVE IN THIS WORLD. SOLOMON WROTE ANOTHER GREAT BOOK IN THE BIBLE CALLED SONG OF SONGS, AND IT'S ABOUT THE LOVE BETWEEN A MAN AND A WOMAN.

YEAH!

IS IT MUSHY? IF IT IS, I DON'T WANT TO HEAR ANOTHER WORD.

THE DIVIDED KINGDOM

Solomon died after being the King of Israel for about forty years. (1 Kings 4:29-34 and 1 Kings 5:1-6:38) After Solomon died, his son Rehoboam was declared King of Israel. Rehoboam did not follow in his father's footsteps and made many bad choices for himself and the kingdom. He chose to listen to his friends who had selfish agendas instead of looking out for the kingdom as a whole. He required the people to pay more taxes, which caused several tribes in the north to break away and create their own kingdom.

Jeroboam became king of the newly formed northern kingdom, called Israel, while Rehoboam continued to rule over the southern kingdom, which became known as Judah.

God had previously warned David that his house would fight against itself and this prophecy had come true. These two kingdoms often fought with each other.

God's kings and their people turned their backs on him and continued to disobey his commandments and for this disobedience, their enemies would eventually take over their lands and place the people in captivity.

KINGS OF JUDAH
[C 925-586 BC]

Jeroboam
Nadab
Baasha
Elah
Zimri
Omri
Ahab
Ahaziah
Jehoram
Jehu
Jehoahaz
Joash
Jeroboam II
Zachariah
Sallum
Menahem
Pekahiah
Pekah
Hoshea

KINGS OF ISRAEL
[C 925-586 BC]

Rehoboam
Abijam
Asa
Jehoshaphat
Jehoram
Ahaziah
Athaliah
Joash
Amaziah
Uzziah
Jotham
Ahaz
Hezekiah
Manasseh
Amon
Josiah
Jehoahaz
Jehoiakim
Jehoiachin
Zedekiah

Sea of Galilee

Mediterranean Sea

ISRAEL

● Jerusalem

JUDAH

Dead Sea

The northern kingdom had many bad kings as its ruler. Some worshiped idols, two were assassinated, and one committed suicide. The seventh king, Omri, named the city of Samaria as the northern kingdom's capital. The eighth king, Ahab, was the most evil king the nation ever had. Ahab refused to have anything to do with God and his statues, and even married a foreign princess named Jezebel, who was a worshiper of Baal, the god of the Canaanites. She influenced Ahab to name Baal as the northern kingdom's official god and commanded all the people to worship him. This greatly displeased God so he sent the prophet Elijah to speak to Ahab.

STAY TOGETHER! WE'VE JUST LEFT JERUSALEM, THE CAPITAL OF THE SOUTHERN KINGDOM, JUDAH.

WE'LL BE SHIFTING BACK TO OUR OWN TIME PERIOD AS WE TRAVEL, SO KEEP YOUR RSPS WITH YOU. I DON'T WANT TO LOSE ANYONE.

HOW COME I HAVE TO RIDE A MINIBIKE?

SORRY ABOUT THAT. WE COULD ONLY FIND SEVEN MOTORCYCLES.

NAMES FOR ISRAEL:

The country where the Israelites lived had several names over the centuries, which can be confusing. The whole country was at first called Canaan or the Promised Land. After the Israelites conquered Canaan, the whole country was called Israel. But after King Solomon's death, the name Israel meant only the ten tribes in the north (the southern part was called Judah). Other names for the whole country are the Holy Land and Palestine.

THE PROPHET ELIJAH

Elijah was a prophet of God who lived in the northern kingdom of Israel. Sometimes he was called the "Tishbite," which might refer to where he grew up. Although Elijah did many things as God's messenger, his most famous incident was at Mount Carmel.

Elijah spoke with King Ahab and told him that no rain would fall in Israel for several years unless he commanded it. After three years without rain, God told Elijah to return to King Ahab to see if his heart had changed. King Ahab, however, had decided to try and make it rain by gathering 450 prophets of Baal together and have them pray to their god.

The prophets of Baal sacrificed a bull and began their religious chants to their god, asking him to answer their prayers. These chants went on for hours. Elijah began to taunt the prophets by asking if their god was asleep or maybe he was on a trip and couldn't hear them. This angered the prophets and they began to chant louder and louder. They began cutting themselves with swords and sharp objects and dancing around, but nothing happened. No response from Baal was heard or seen.

When the prophets had stopped, Elijah built an altar with twelve stones, each representing one of the twelve tribes of Israel. He stacked wood around the altar and requested that water be poured all over the wood. He also asked that a trench be dug around the altar and filled with water. Then Elijah prayed a simple prayer to God who sent fire from heaven that consumed the sacrifice, the wood, and all of the water.

This powerful display of God's power convinced the people of Israel that God was real and they turned back to worshiping him.

When it was time for Elijah's life to end, he did not die as other people do, but was taken up into heaven in a chariot of fire. This would have been a great sight to see.
(1 Kings 18: 20-46)

WHAT IS A PROPHET?

A prophet is a man chosen by God to deliver a message to mankind. Often, prophets would give messages to kings and other times, to the nation as a whole. Most of these messages were about their behavior or disobedience to God. The prophets proclaimed warnings and asked the people to turn from their evil ways and follow God.

WHO IS BAAL?

The Canaanites were the original inhabitants of the Promised Land that God gave to Abraham. They believed in several gods such as Baal, whom we read a lot about in the Old Testament. Baal was the storm god who was believed to be able to control the rain, thunder, and lightening. Many statues have been found of Baal, usually holding a thunderbolt. The Canaanites would pray to Baal asking that he water their crops.

THE PROPHET ELISHA

Elisha was a prophet who is sometimes confused with Elijah. Elijah found Elisha while he was plowing a field and asked him to follow. Following Elijah's death, Elisha took his place and performed many miracles in the name of God. Like Elijah, Elisha continued to warn the people of God that the way they were living their lives would only end in destruction. He warned of God's judgment and demonstrated God's message in some unique ways.

One time, Elisha and some friends were chopping wood, and an iron axe-head fell in the water. Tools were made by hand and very expensive. Elisha threw a piece of wood in the water and the axe-head came floating up! (2 Kings 6:1-7)

Later, Elisha helped the king of Israel to defeat the army of the king of Aram.

WE'RE HEADING BACK IN TIME TO THE JORDAN RIVER, WHERE ELIJAH TOOK HIS GLORIOUS CHARIOT RIDE.

JUST BEFORE HE DID, HE SLAPPED THE RIVER WITH HIS CLOAK, AND IT PARTED. AFTER HE LEFT, ELISHA PICKED UP ELIJAH'S CLOAK AND STRUCK THE RIVER TOO, AND THE WATER PARTED AGAIN. THAT'S HOW THE PEOPLE KNEW THAT GOD HAD CHOSEN ELISHA TO TAKE ELIJAH'S PLACE.

COOL! ARE YOU GOING TO GIVE US A WATER-PARTING DEMONSTRATION?

SORRY, I LEFT MY CLOAK AT HOME ... ANYWAY, WE'RE SHOOTING FOR A TIME A LITTLE WHILE AFTER THAT SCENE. JOSH AND I WANT TO SHOW YOU ANOTHER OF ELISHA'S MIRACLES THAT HAPPENED AT THE JORDAN RIVER.

The Arameans tried to attack the northern kingdom many times, but each time Elisha would tell the king of Israel where the Arameans would attack next, so the king was always prepared. The king of Aram finally figured out what Elisha was doing and wanted to kill him. When he heard that Elisha was in the city of Dothan, the Aramean army surrounded the city at night. But Elisha wasn't worried. He asked God to make the army of Aram blind, and then he walked out to meet them. He told the Arameans that they were in the wrong place and offered to take them to the right place. He took them right into Samaria, the capital of the northern kingdom. The Arameans thought they were dead for sure, but Elisha told the king of Samaria to let them go – after they had been treated to a big feast. And the Arameans quit bothering Israel, at least for a while. (2 Kings 6-8-23)

You can read more about the miracles Elisha performed in 2 Kings 6: 1-7, 2 Kings 4:1-7 and 4:8-37.

naaman

One of the generals of the Aramean army, Naaman, had leprosy—a terrible disease that couldn't be cured. His wife had an Israelite servant girl who told her about Elisha.

So Naaman went to see Elisha. At first Elisha thought this was a trick, but God told him to help. Elisha told Naaman to wash himself seven times in the Jordan River—and Naaman wasn't happy about it! But his servants begged him to try, so he did, grumbling the entire time. No surprise to us, he was cured, and from that day on, Naaman promised Elisha that he would never worship any god but the Lord. (2 Kings 5:1-27)

Naaman, a foreigner, turned to the Lord, but many kings of Israel did not. One king after another ignored God and disobeyed God's law. God sent several other prophets, like Amos and Hosea, but nothing helped.

Finally, there was no turning back. The people refused to listen. Their hearts became hardened. God had plans that involved the Assyrians—and those plans weren't pretty.

DID YOU KNOW THAT THIS MAN WAS HEALED OF HIS TERRIBLE DISEASE BECAUSE OF A SERVANT GIRL?

SHE BOLDLY SPOKE UP AND SAID HE SHOULD COME TO ISRAEL AND SEE THE PROPHET ELISHA. ELISHA TOLD HIM WHAT TO DO, AND THE REST IS HISTORY.

HERE AT THE JORDAN RIVER IS THE MIRACLE JOSH AND I WANTED TO SHOW YOU. IT'S A GREAT EXAMPLE OF HOW A YOUNG PERSON CAN MAKE A BIG DIFFERENCE.

THAT'S SO GREAT!

SHE REALLY DID MAKE A DIFFERENCE.

WHY DO THESE THINGS ALWAYS HAPPEN TO ME?

ASSYRIANS

Over the course of two centuries, a large nation—an empire—had been growing in the east: Assyria. The Assyrians liked war. They went out each year to fight, not because they wanted or needed more land, but because they needed money and

slaves to build their great cities – especially Nineveh, their capital. They were a very cruel people. When we talk about taking a "head count" we mean counting people. In war, the Assyrians would do a literal head count. Soldiers would bring the heads of the enemies they killed to be counted.

JONAH

Jonah was a prophet whom God asked to deliver a message of judgment to the Assyrian people because of their evil ways. Jonah was told to travel to Nineveh, a major Assyrian city, and tell the people that the city would be destroyed in forty days if they did not change their behavior and turn to God.

The Assyrians had been enemies of Israel and other nations for many years. In fact, the Assyrians went to war each year just to bring back slaves and objects of value to use in developing their nation. No one liked the Assyrians.

Now God was asking Jonah to go to the people of Assyria and warn them if they did not change, they would be destroyed. Jonah did not want them to have a chance to obey God and be forgiven; he wanted Nineveh to be destroyed. So Jonah chose not to obey God and instead of going to Nineveh, Jonah went the opposite direction, to the west, because Nineveh was east.

Not too long into his voyage, a huge storm began to blow. The storm tossed the ship

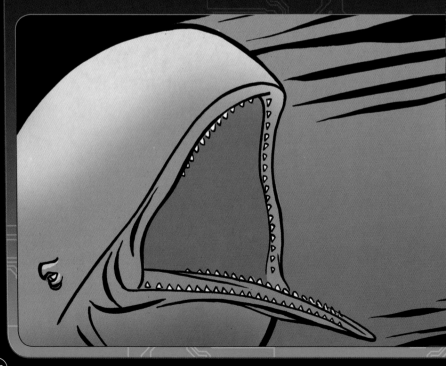

around until it was about to break apart. Jonah knew the storm had been sent by God to remind him that he was going in the wrong direction. Jonah told the sailors what he knew and the sailors decided to throw him overboard in order to save the ship.

Jonah did not know if he would live or die as he hit the water; however, God still wanted Jonah to go to Nineveh. God sent a great fish to swallow Jonah and he remained in the belly of the fish for three days. Finally Jonah agreed to go to Nineveh and the fish threw him up on the beach. Jonah looked terrible. He headed to Nineveh where he preached God's warning to the Assyrian people. Much to Jonah's dislike, the people of Assyria repented of their behavior and turned to God and the city was spared from destruction.

Unfortunately, the Assyrians were not faithful to God for long and turned back to their old behaviors. Once again the Assyrians began to attack other nations and eventually conquered Israel and took the people as slaves. This was the last time anyone had seen or heard of the northern kingdom of Israel. (Jonah 1-4)

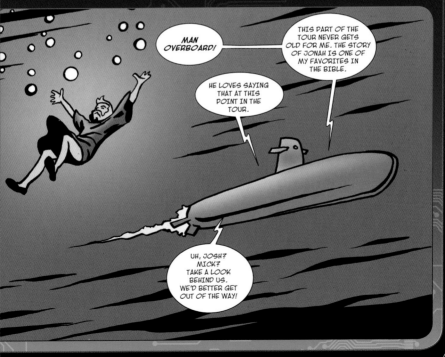

JUDAH: THE SOUTHERN KINGDOM

The kings of the northern kingdom of Israel had not followed the Lord, but some in the southern kingdom of Judah had. Some of the kings of Judah followed the commandments of God and some didn't. Much like Israel to the north, Judah in general did not fear God as they once had done. One of the best kings that ruled in Judah since the time of David and Solomon was Hezekiah. Hezekiah was a righteous man and followed God's rules as best he could. He abolished worshiping idols, destroyed the sacred sites that were associated with idol worship, and led the people to worship the God of Israel.

THE BOOKS OF KINGS & CHRONICLES

The books of 1 & 2 Kings record the time of Solomon's reign, events related to the prophets Elijah and Elisha, and various events that occurred in the northern and southern kingdoms. Similarly, the books of 1 & 2 Chronicles are also historical, and they include the genealogy of King David's family. These books cover the timeframe from the fall of Adam in Genesis to Solomon's reign and beyond.

DAVID

SOLOMON

WHICH IS GOOD, SINCE OUR NEXT STOP IS BACK IN JERUSALEM. THAT CITY REMAINED THE CAPITAL OF THE SOUTHERN KINGDOM AFTER KING SOLOMON DIED.

I THINK MY MULE'S DEFECTIVE.

HEZEKIAH

One of the best kings that ruled in Judah since the time of David and Solomon was Hezekiah. One of Hezekiah's friends was the prophet Isaiah. Hezekiah was a righteous man and followed God's rules as best he could. He abolished worshiping idols, destroyed the sacred sites that were associated with idol worship, and led the people to worship the God of Israel.

ISAIAH

Isaiah was a prophet who preached against ungodliness and idolatry. He was disliked by most who heard him, especially the corrupt kings, because he reminded the people that God was watching and displeased with the type of lives they were living. God showed Isaiah a vision, and Isaiah saw the Lord sitting on his throne being worshiped by Seraphim, or angels. Throughout the book, Isaiah presents evidence of the coming Messiah and Gospel of Jesus Christ. Much of the book of Isaiah is made up of prophecies that were to come true later in Israel's life. Isaiah, along with Jeremiah, Ezekiel, and Daniel are known as the Major Prophets because their books are longer than the Minor Prophets.

LOOK, I FOUND A CLUE! IT'S A MESSAGE FROM DAD ON A YELLOW STICKY NOTE.

THAT'S WEIRD!

IT SAYS, "DAD WAS HERE."

THAT IS WEIRD. YOUR FATHER CARRIES STICKY NOTES AROUND WITH HIM?

Jeremiah was known as the "weeping" prophet because of his sadness over how the people of Israel had turned away from God. He was a prophet whom God sent to the people of Judah and is credited with writing not only the book of Jeremiah, which bears his name, but Lamentations and 1 & 2 Kings as well. Jeremiah's ministry lasted about forty years and, like Isaiah, he preached against the nations' idolatry and warned them to return to the God who had called their forefathers out of the land of Egypt. Sadly, Jeremiah also foretold of the destruction of Jerusalem by the Babylonians that would occur in 586 BC. (2 Kings 22:1-11; 23:1-3)

Jeremiah explains that he was called by the Lord to be his prophet even before he was conceived in his mother's womb. He was commanded to speak to the people God's words, even though he felt himself too young. In verse 6, he shares that he questioned God's choice. "Behold, I do not know how to speak, because I am a youth." But God replies, "Do not say, 'I am a youth,' because everywhere I send you, you shall go, and all that I command you, you shall speak." Jeremiah did as God asked and spent his life as a mouthpiece for God. (Jeremiah 1:4-10, NASB)

Jeremiah's job was not easy, because many times he had to speak words that were not favorable to his audience's hearing. In this instance, Jeremiah is telling King Zedekiah and his advisors that everyone in the city should leave and go out from the walls before the Babylonian army burned the city and killed the people. King Zedekiah's advisors did not like what they were hearing and asked if they could put Jeremiah to death for the words he had spoken. The king allowed them to take care of Jeremiah. These men took him to a cistern (well) and placed him at the bottom. They left him with no food and water to die.

Read Jeremiah 38:1-16 to find out what happened to Jeremiah.

ADVENTURE READINGS

Jeremiah 1:4-19

Jeremiah 26:1-24

Jeremiah 37:1-21

Jeremiah 38:1-13

Jeremiah 52:1-16

In 722 BC the Assyrians conquered the northern kingdom of Israel. Many of the people who made up the ten tribes that lived in the northern kingdom were taken into captivity and never heard from again. Since that time, another nation, called the Babylonians, had grown into an even bigger nation. They destroyed the Assyrians, who had attacked Israel, and were ready to conquer the southern kingdom of Judah.

Babylon was located in a plain near the Tigris and Euphrates Rivers, which was a great place to grow food. Under the leadership of King Nebuchadnezzar, the nation grew in size and built many buildings that were considered great accomplishments of the time. The Babylonians also helped in the development of subjects such as mathematics, astronomy, geography, and medicine.

Just as God had promised, he used the Babylonians to judge the people of Judah because of their rebellion against him. As a result, the Babylonians took the people of Judah into captivity and brought them to Babylon where they stayed for seventy years, until God decided to let them go back to Israel. (2 Kings 24:8-2 Kings 25:12)

The word "lamentations" refers to sorrow or grief over something. As such, the book of Lamentations is a long, sad poem of grief about Israel's refusal to follow God's laws. It is also a request that God not turn His back on the Israelite people, but forgive them. Lamentations records Jeremiah's sadness about the Babylonians, who were coming to destroy Jerusalem and the southern kingdom of Judah.

After the Babylonians had conquered the area of Judah, the people were captured and taken back to Babylon just as God had warned. Babylon was a large country that lay between two great rivers, the Euphrates River and the Tigris River. It was in this area that the people of Judah would spend the next seventy years of their life.

Babylon was the capital city in the Babylonian kingdom. It was founded by Nimrod many years ago and was the location where the Tower of Babel had been built. Today Babylon is located in the country of Iraq. The ruler during the time of Judah's capture was King Nebuchadnezzar. This king liked grand things and had many temples and palaces built in the kingdom. One of the more special places Nebuchadnezzar had built was called the Hanging Gardens. This unique garden had many terraces that were filled with beautiful plants. Today, the Hanging Gardens of Babylon is one of the Seven Wonders of the World.

Fun Fact: In the city of Babylon was a huge ziggurat, which may have been the original Tower of Babel.

Daniel

One of the slaves whom King Nebuchadnezzar's army captured was a young boy named Daniel. Because Daniel was very smart, he, and others like him, was brought to live in Babylon in the king's court. Even though Daniel was in captivity he continued to follow God's laws.

One day, King Nebuchadnezzar had a dream about a statue made of different types of materials. None of his advisors, or those who claimed to understand dreams, was able to tell the king the meaning of his dream. Daniel heard what was happening and offered to interpret the dream. Daniel explained that the statue the king had seen represented different kingdoms that were to come to power in the future. The head of the statue was made of gold and represented Babylon. The second kingdom was the chest and arms that were made of silver and represented the Medo-Persian Empire. The third kingdom, represented by the belly and thighs of the statue, was made of

bronze and would be the Greek empire. And the last kingdom, the legs were made of iron, with the feet made of both iron and clay. This kingdom was not named, but it was described as more evil than the others. Daniel explained that God was going to someday destroy these four nations represented by the statue and set up his own kingdom that would last forever.

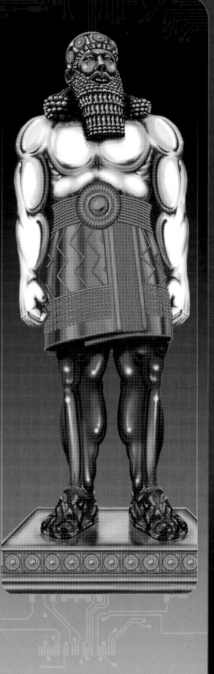

CHECK OUT THAT GOLD STATUE!

MAYBE WE COULD SNEAK OVER AND BREAK OFF A TOE. THAT WOULD BE WORTH A LOT BACK HOME.

WE'RE IN A TIME-WARP BUBBLE, REMEMBER? WE CAN'T TAKE ANYTHING HOME FROM THE PAST.

Daniel in the Lion's Den

After King Nebuchadnezzar died, King Darius took his place. King Darius continued to use Daniel as one of his prominent advisors even though he knew that Daniel served God. The other advisors to the king did not like Daniel and devised a plan to get rid of him. They knew that Daniel prayed daily to God, so the advisors convinced King Darius to pass a law that no one could pray to any god for one month except to King Darius. Because Daniel was faithful, he continued to pray to God despite the new law. The advisors told King Darius about Daniel's disobedience. King Darius questioned Daniel and because Daniel admitted that he had broken the law, King Darius had to punish him. So he threw Daniel into a den of lions.

The next morning, King Darius ran to the lion's den to check on Daniel and found that Daniel had survived the night without a scratch. God had protected Daniel from the lions. King Darius was angry with his advisors and ordered that they be thrown into the lion's den. Unlike Daniel's experience, the lions killed the advisors immediately.

Daniel continued to serve as King Darius' main advisor throughout his reign and also served under the next king, King Cyrus. (Daniel 1-12)

EZEKIEL

Ezekiel was one of God's prophets who was also taken to Babylon with the first group of people. Like Jeremiah and Isaiah, Ezekiel reminded the people that each person was responsible for his/her own actions. Ezekiel is known for his strange vision of God that is recorded in Ezekiel 1:1-28. His vision included different types of wheels moving in various directions and of four living creatures. His vision has also been compared to some of John's visions which he described in the book of Revelation. Ezekiel was also given vision about dry bones coming to life which represented God's people coming back into their land and of a new temple that had yet to be built. (Ezekiel 37:1-14)

QUEEN ESTHER

During the time of the Persian Empire, just after the Babylonians ruled, there lived a young woman named Esther. The king at that time was King Ahasuerus, and he was married to a Queen named Vashti. Queen Vashti was known for her beauty. Unfortunately, one day King Ahasuerus became angry with the queen because she refused to obey one of his commands. As a result, Queen Vashti was removed from her position and King Ahasuerus began looking for a new queen. After searching throughout the kingdom, King Ahasuerus chose Esther to be his new queen. Unknown to Esther at the time, God would use her new position to save the people of Israel.

Sometime later, Esther heard about a plot to have all of the Jewish people in the land killed. Esther went before the King and asked his permission to allow the Jewish people to defend themselves, which he did. In addition, the men who had plotted to kill the Jewish people were captured and killed. God used Esther to save her people from destruction. (Esther 1-10)

HURRY, HURRY, YOU'RE GOING TO MISS IT! WE WANT TO SHOW YOU ONE MORE GREAT THING THAT HAPPENED WHILE THE ISRAELITES WERE IN THIS FOREIGN LAND.

WHICH IS NOW PART OF THE PERSIAN EMPIRE, BY THE WAY, BECAUSE WE'VE MOVED FORWARD IN TIME...

BUT ANYWAY, ESTHER IS RISKING HER LIFE BY ENTERING THE KING'S THRONE ROOM WITHOUT AN INVITATION. IF HE RAISES HIS SCEPTER, SHE CAN GO TALK TO HIM. IF NOT, SHE'S TOAST.

I CAN'T TAKE THIS SUSPENSE...

BACK IN JERUSALEM

During the seventy years while the Jewish people were held captive in Babylon, the Persians conquered the Babylonian Empire and rose to power. Under King Cyrus' rule, many of the Jews were allowed to return to Jerusalem. It is estimated that over 40,000 people left Babylon, but many others decided to stay where they had already built a life. While the Jewish people were in exile, other nations had taken over their land and when they returned, conflicts arose.

As the Jewish people began rebuilding the temple, some became distracted. Although the prophets Haggai and Zechariah encouraged the people to continue building the temple and the city walls, it still took twenty years to complete. (Ezra 3:7-6:18)

ADVENTURE READINGS

Esther 2:1-23

Esther 3

Esther 4:1-5:8

Esther 6, 7, 8

HE'S RAISING HIS SCEPTER! YAY, SHE'S GOING TO BE ALL RIGHT!

THAT TOOK A LOT OF GUTS.

AND FAITH.

WHY DID SHE TAKE SUCH A BIG RISK?

BECAUSE SHE'S A JEW, AND SHE LEARNED THAT SOME BAD PEOPLE WERE PLOTTING TO KILL ALL OF HER PEOPLE. BUT NOW, THANKS TO ESTHER, THEY'LL ALL BE SAFE.

NEHEMIAH

Nehemiah was a man of God who was in the service of King Artaxerxes. One day while the king was served his wine, King Artaxerxes noticed Nehemiah's mood and asked him what was wrong. Nehemiah told King Artaxerxes that he was sad because he had heard from a friend that the city of Jerusalem was in ruins. Nehemiah asked the king if he would send him back to Jerusalem to help rebuild the city. King Artaxerxes granted Nehemiah's request and allowed him to return to Jerusalem to head up the rebuilding project. Nehemiah and other workers returned to Jerusalem and began to rebuild the walls of the city. (Nehemiah 2-3)

LET'S LIVE IT

When we pray for God to help us, God doesn't expect us to sit back and do nothing. Nehemiah prayed, and then set guards and worked as hard as he could. If, for example, you have a test, ask for God's help and study as hard as you can.

OTHER PROPHETS

In addition to Isaiah, Jeremiah, Ezekiel, and Daniel, there were many other prophets who spoke for God and whose stories are told in the pages of the Old Testament. Below is a list of the prophets who served God. For more information on each of these prophets, read the chapters listed.

Hosea (Hosea 1-14)

Joel (Joel 3)

Amos (Amos 1-9)

Obadiah (Obadiah 1:1-21)

Micah (Micah 1-7)

Nahum (Nahum 1-3)

Habakkuk (Habakkuk 1-3)

Zephaniah (Zephaniah 1-3)

Haggai (Haggai 1-2)

Zechariah (Zechariah 1-14)

Malachi (Malachi 1-4)

BETWEEN THE OLD & NEW TESTAMENTS

At the end of the Old Testament, the Persian Empire was in control. There was only a small temple in Jerusalem and Judah did not have a king. As we enter the New Testament, we discover that a new temple has been built in Jerusalem, that there is a leader named Herod who serves as a king over the land, and that the Jews have begun to meet in what are called Synagogues. There are also several new Jewish groups that had developed since the time of the Old Testament. The two most important of these groups were the Pharisees and the Sadducees, whom Jesus would encounter many times during his time on earth.

About four hundred years separate the events and people of the Old Testament from the New Testament. Although the Bible does not say anything about what happened during this time, other historical books give us information about what occurred.

Some of the books that tell about the time between the Testaments are called the Apocrypha; these books are included in the Catholic Bible.

THE OLD TESTAMENT

The Old Testament is made up of thirty-nine different books written over a long period of time by many different people. The books of the Old Testament are divided into the following sections:

PENTATEUCH – Genesis, Exodus, Leviticus, Numbers, and Deuteronomy

HISTORICAL BOOKS - Joshua, Judges, Ruth, I & 2 Samuel, I & 2 Kings, I & 2 Chronicles, Ezra, Nehemiah, and Esther

POETIC BOOKS – Job, Psalms, Proverbs, Ecclesiastes, and Song of Solomon

MAJOR PROPHETS – Isaiah, Jeremiah, Lamentations, Ezekiel, and Daniel

MINOR PROPHETS – Hosea, Joel, Amos, Obadiah, Jonah, Micah, Nahum, Habakkuk, Zephaniah, Haggai, Zechariah, and Malachi

SYNAGOGUES

When the children of Israel wandered in the wilderness for forty years, they worshiped God in a moveable tabernacle. Later, King Solomon built a permanent structure in Jerusalem called the temple. This is where all of the people were to gather to worship God before the New Testament synagogues were invented. These were places much like the church buildings you see today. Every town built a synagogue where the Jewish people met to read the scriptures and pray together.

PHARISEES & SADDUCEES

The Pharisees and the Sadducees were the two most important Jewish groups in the New Testament. But what is the difference between a Pharisee and a Sadducee? The Pharisees were religious leaders in Israel who did not embrace the Greek culture and who were very concerned to follow the laws of God. The Sadducees were also religious leaders but who did not view the Greek culture as a bad thing. They were very involved in the politics of the day and were very concerned with gaining power in the Roman empire, which ruled during this time.

BETWEEN THE OLD & NEW TESTAMENTS

SAMARITANS

Samaritans were the people who lived in Samaria, an area of land located between Judea to the south and Galilee to the north. The Samaritans were part Jew and part Gentile. The Samaritan people worshiped God, but they worshiped him on the Mount Gerizim instead of Jerusalem. The Jewish people did not like the Samaritans and thought they were beneath them in status. In fact, the Jews disliked the Samaritans so much that they would often refer to the Samaritans as "dogs."

SANHEDRIN

The Sanhedrin was a group of seventy-one Jewish religious leaders who were made up of Pharisees and Sadducees. The Sanhedrin controlled civil and religious matters in the daily lives of the Israelites. The high priest was given the position of authority of the Sanhedrin. It was this group of leaders who sentenced Jesus Christ to death.

UH-OH, JJ. SOMETHING'S WRONG.

I KNOW WE WEREN'T WITH THE GROUP WHEN THEY DID A TIME-JUMP, BUT ALL OF OUR RSPS ARE SUPPOSED TO WORK TOGETHER.

WHY DIDN'T WE GO TOO? UNLESS...

IT'S JUST WHAT I WAS AFRAID OF. MY RSP BROKE WHEN I FELL.

OH NO, JJ! WE'RE GONNA BE TRAPPED HERE FOREVER!

KING HEROD THE GREAT

At the time Jesus was born, Herod the Great was king of Palestine, which was the same area as the Promised Land. Herod liked to build beautiful structures to live in. He built a palace on the top of a large mountain called Masada and a fortress that was made by cutting out the top of another mountain. Herod even built a city by the sea called Caesarea. Some of his projects took many years to build. And some of his projects can still be seen today if you visit the land of Israel.

Herod was not Jewish, nor was he a very religious man, so he attempted to make the people of Israel like him by rebuilding the temple in Jerusalem. The temple was perhaps his greatest achievement. It was a magnificent structure that could be seen from miles around. Unfortunately, the temple was destroyed in 70 AD when the Roman army attacked the city of Jerusalem. Although the walls no longer stand, the foundation of the temple, called the Temple Mount, can still be seen. In fact, the western side of the foundation is today called the Wailing Wall.

Herod was so suspicious and jealous of other people that he killed even his own wife and his two sons because he thought they wanted him dead.

WHAT DOES "GOSPEL" MEAN?

Since the time when Adam and Eve disobeyed God in the Garden of Eden, every person has failed to keep the laws and commandments of God completely. Because of this, in the Old Testament the people had to sacrifice different animals throughout the year to atone for their sins. However, God promised that one day he would send a deliverer, or Messiah, who would replace the Old Testament sacrificial system. Throughout the Old Testament, the people looked for the Messiah that was promised, but they never found him. As the New Testament begins, we learn about the baby Jesus who was to fulfill the promise and be the savior of the world.

Sadly, many of the people were looking for a powerful ruler and not a little baby to be the savior of Israel. Many had a hard time accepting that Jesus Christ was the Messiah whom God had promised to send so long ago. But for those who did believe, the coming of Jesus into the world was good news.

And that is the meaning of the word "gospel," good news. The good news of the gospel is that God has taken care of the problem of sin by sending His only son to be our sacrifice once for all. Jesus was sent to teach and be the ultimate sacrifice for the sins of the world.

WHY ARE THERE FOUR GOSPELS?

The New Testament books of Matthew, Mark, Luke, and John record eyewitness accounts of those who heard Jesus teach and lived with him. These four books are also called the Gospels because they contain the good news about Jesus and what he came to do for mankind. Each book tells us something different about Jesus' life and together gives us a full picture of who Jesus was and what he taught.

MATTHEW – written for the Jews and demonstrates that Jesus fulfilled many prophecies about the Messiah in his life.

MARK – written for those who are not familiar with who Jesus is. It is thought to be the first book written of the four books.

LUKE – written by a physician, this book records Jesus' family line and gives us a lot of historical background to Jesus' life.

JOHN – different from the other three, John uses simple words to show that Jesus was in fact the Son of God.

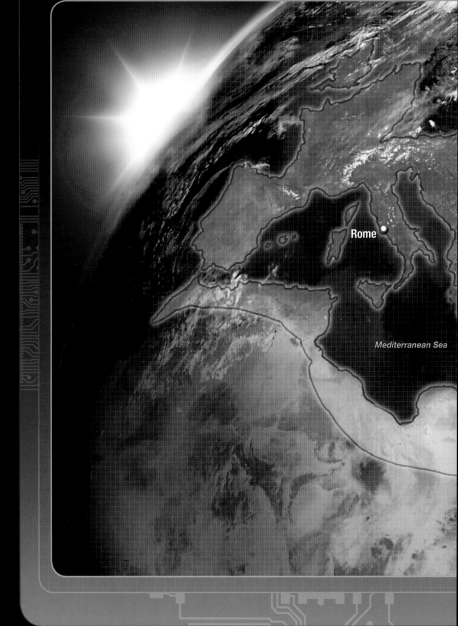

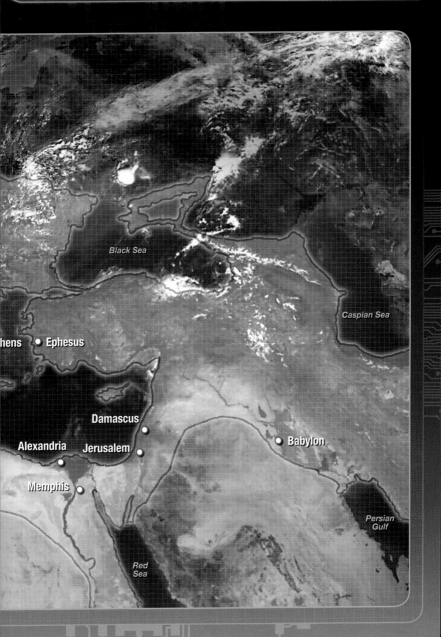

JESUS' BIRTH

ZECHARIAH

Zechariah was a priest who served in the temple just before the time when Jesus was born. One day an angel of the Lord appeared to Zechariah and told him that he and his wife would soon have a child and that he would be a mighty prophet of God. Zechariah questioned the angel because he and his wife were very old and past the age of having children. The angel told Zechariah that due to his disbelief he would not be able to talk again until his promised son was born.

On the day his son was born, Zechariah wrote down the name the angel had told him to call the child, John. After Zechariah wrote the name, he was able to speak again. John became a messenger for God and pointed others to Jesus the Messiah.

(Luke 1:1-25, 57-80)

MARY

Mary was a young woman who lived in Nazareth. One night an angel visited
Mary and told her that she would have a baby boy. Mary was troubled because
she was not married but only engaged to Joseph. The angel told Mary that
she had been chosen by God to give birth to the Son of God and that his name
would be Jesus. Mary believed the angel and trusted God to take care of her.
(Matthew 1:19-2:23; Luke 1:26-56)

JOSEPH

Joseph was a young carpenter who lived in the small town of Nazareth. He was
engaged to be married to Mary when he learned that she was going to have a baby.
After an angel visited him, Joseph trusted God and took Mary as his wife.

Soon after this time, it was proclaimed that a census be taken of all the people who
lived in the Roman Empire. Everyone was to travel to the town where their family
originated. For Mary and Joseph, this was Bethlehem.

When Mary and Joseph arrived in Bethlehem, they were unable to find a room to stay in because there were so many visitors in town for the census. After searching everywhere, the only place they could find to stay was a stable where the animals were kept. It was here, in a barn, that Mary gave birth to her son Jesus. That same night, shepherds, who were watching their flocks of sheep in the fields, were told of the birth by a host of angels. Immediately, the shepherds hurried to find the baby. They marveled at what they saw and worshiped the promised Messiah who had been born to save Israel. **(Matthew 1:18-25; Luke 2:1-21)**

THIS IS WHAT IT'S ALL ABOUT, GUYS...

THE BIBLE SAYS THAT GOD LOVES US ALL SO MUCH THAT HE GAVE HIS ONLY SON, SO THAT IF WE BELIEVE IN HIM, WE WON'T DIE BECAUSE OF OUR SINS. INSTEAD WE'LL LIVE WITH GOD FOREVER!

HEROD HEARS OF THE NEW KING

The Magi were a group of men who studied, understood the times in which they lived, and recognized the sign that the Messiah had been born. The sign was a bright star that stood in the sky over the place where the Messiah had been born. When they saw the star, they traveled from the east to find the new king. When the wise men came to Jerusalem, they stopped to ask King Herod about the new king's birth. King Herod did not know of this prophesy or where the baby was born, so he asked his advisors. The wise men continued on their journey to find the child and when they arrived at the home of Mary and Joseph, they began to worship the child and presented him with gifts of gold, frankincense, and myrrh.

Meanwhile, King Herod had gathered together all of his advisors to learn more about the Messiah who was to be born. When he discovered that the child was to be born in Bethlehem, King Herod sent an order to kill all babies two years old and under in the Bethlehem area. Herod did this because he was afraid that Jesus would someday become king of Judah and take his place. (Matthew 2:1-12)

JESUS - AGE 12

Jesus grew up with many brothers and sisters and took on the profession of a carpenter like his earthly father, Joseph. When Jesus was twelve, his family went to Jerusalem to worship God at the temple. As they were traveling back home from Jerusalem, Joseph and Mary realized that Jesus was not with them and had been left behind. Joseph and Mary headed back to Jerusalem as quick as they could. When they entered the courtyard of the temple, they found Jesus sitting with the teachers of the law.

Jesus asked many questions and the religious leaders were amazed at his knowledge. His parents asked Jesus why he had stayed behind and he replied, "Why is it that you were looking for me? Did you not know that I had to be in My Father's house?" (Luke 2:41-52, NASB)

JOHN THE BAPTIST

Following some unique events surrounding his birth, John grew to be a mighty man of God. He lived in the wilderness until God called him to begin preaching around the Jordan area. His message was simple, "Repent, for the kingdom of heaven is near!"

John wore clothes made of camel's hair and a leather belt and was known for eating locusts and honey. Even though he may have seemed like a strange person, many people from Jerusalem came to listen to his message. Those who accepted his message were baptized by John and this is why he is called John the Baptist.

John preached to huge crowds, warning them of their need to repent from their sins and return to God. He also told the people about a special person who was soon to come. John proclaimed that this individual would save the people from their sins. John was careful not to be confused with the Messiah and often told the people that he was not the Messiah.

One day, when John was preaching and baptizing, he saw Jesus and immediately recognized him as the one whom God had sent, the Messiah. Before all the people, John proclaimed loudly, "Behold, the lamb of God, who takes away the sin of the world." (John 1:29-31; Mathew 3:13-17, ESV)

JESUS' BAPTISM

One day Jesus came to where John the Baptist was baptizing many people and asked to be baptized. John, knowing who Jesus was, replied that he did not feel worthy of the task, but that Jesus should baptize him. Jesus explained to John that he needed to be baptized to fulfill the calling God had placed on his life. John obeyed and baptized Jesus.

When Jesus came out of the water from being baptized, the Holy Spirit descended upon him in the form of a dove and a voice from heaven proclaimed, "This is my beloved Son, with whom I am well pleased." This was the first event in Jesus' ministry. (Matthew 3:13-17, ESV)

ADVENTURE READINGS

Luke 3:19-20   Luke 17:20, 21

Matthew 14:1-13   John 18:36-37

Luke 9:46-48

JESUS' MINISTRY BEGINS

THE DISCIPLES ARE CALLED

Early in Jesus' ministry, he began to call his disciples. Andrew had previously been a disciple of John but began to follow Jesus with his brother Peter, after meeting Jesus. When the three journeyed into Galilee, Philip and Nathanael, who is also called Bartholomew, were added to the group. Next, Jesus encountered two brothers, James and John, who were fishing and called them to follow him. Matthew was collecting taxes when Jesus asked him to leave his job and follow him. Other disciples who were added, who would eventually become the twelve apostles, were Thomas, Judas the son of James, Judas of Iscariot, Simon, and James. Of all the disciples, it was Judas of Iscariot who would betray Jesus.

WHO WERE THE DISCIPLES?

Andrew – A previous disciple of John the Baptist, he was out fishing when Jesus approached him. (John 1:40 & Matthew 4:18)

Peter – He was the brother of Andrew. Jesus changed his name from Simon to Cephas, which is translated as Peter. (John 1:41)

Philip – He was from Bethsaida. (John 1:43)

James – Little is known about this disciple except that his father's name was Alphaeus. This disciple was not the one who wrote the book of James in the New Testament – that was Jesus' brother, who was also a disciple. (Matthew 10:3; Mark 3:18; Luke 6:15 & Acts 1:13)

Nathaniel – Known as Bartholomew, Nathaniel was a friend of Philip, who had been looking for the Messiah. (John 1:45)

James – He was John's brother and one of the sons of Zebedee. He and his brother John were mending their fishing nets when Jesus asked them to follow him. (Matthew 4:21)

John – Brother to James and another son of Zebedee. He was also a fisherman. (Matthew 4:21)

Simon – Also known as Simon the Zealot. Not much else is known about Simon other than that he is mentioned in the list of disciples' names. (Luke 6: 15)

Matthew – Matthew was previously called Levi and was a tax collector. Matthew was sitting at a table gathering money one day when Jesus walked by and said "Follow me." Matthew arose, left the table, and followed Jesus from that day on. (Luke 5:27-30)

Thomas – Thomas is known as Doubting Thomas because he did not believe the testimony of the other disciples concerning Jesus' resurrection. Thomas stated that he would only believe if he saw Jesus for himself. Jesus did appear to Thomas and asked him to feel his wounds and believe. (John 20:19-29)

Judas – Judas was also referred to as Thaddeus Nathanael or the son of James. There is not much known about him. (John 14:22)

Judas of Iscariot – Judas was the treasurer, or money keeper, for the disciples. He was the disciple who betrayed Jesus to the Roman authorities for thirty pieces of silver. Judas kissed Jesus on the cheek in the Garden of Gethsemane, which led to his arrest. Later, Judas kills himself over his guilt. (Mark 14:44-46)

THE PARABLES OF JESUS

WHAT ARE PARABLES? Parables are short stories about everyday life that include a moral or spiritual lesson. Jesus used parables often in his ministry to teach the people who surrounded him. Many of the parables that he taught are recorded in the four Gospels: Matthew, Mark, Luke, and John.

This was a story Jesus told about two sons who lived with their father. One day, the younger son asked his father for his share of his inheritance. His father gave him what he asked for and the young man left to wander the country. While gone, he squandered all his money on frivolous things until he was broke. In order to survive, the young man took a job on a farm feeding pigs. Quickly he realized that he would be better off as a servant in his father's house than to be working where he was. So he decided to go home. The father saw his son coming up the road and ran to embrace him. The young man apologized to his father for wasting his money and his father forgave him. The father then called for a party to be prepared to celebrate his son returning home. Meanwhile, the older son, who had stayed home to work on the farm, heard what was happening and became angry because his brother was getting so much attention for his bad behavior. His father explained that he had always been with him and would enjoy his inheritance soon, but that they needed to be happy that his brother had been returned to the family. Jesus explained that this was like a person not knowing God and then understanding and believing in Him.

(Luke 15:11-32)

THE PARABLE OF THE SOWER

Jesus told a parable about a man sowing, or planting, seeds in different types of soil. Some seeds were sown by the road, some in rocky places, some among thorns, and some in plowed soil. When Jesus explained the parable, he said that the story illustrated how people accept the gospel. As with proclaiming the gospel about what Jesus did for mankind, the message can fall in many different locations and will be received in different ways. In some the message will take root and bear fruit, but in others it will not. Jesus said that if "anyone hears the word of the kingdom and does not understand it, the evil one comes and snatches away what has been sown in his heart." **(Matthew 13:18-23, ESV)**

THE GOOD SAMARITAN

Jesus told a parable about a man who was travelling from Jerusalem to Jericho and was attacked by robbers. They beat him, took all of his possessions, and then left him for dead on the side of the road. Later, a priest came by the man but moved to the other side of the road to avoid becoming involved. Next a Levite passed by, but he also moved to the other side. Last, a Samaritan came by and saw the man and stopped to help. He took the injured man to an inn, cleaned his wounds, and paid for the man's lodgings until he recovered. Once he had finished the story, Jesus turned to the crowd around him and said, "Which of these three, do you think, proved to be a neighbor to the man who fell among the robbers?" Through this parable, Jesus was showing the people how to treat one another in everyday life.
(Luke 10:30-37, ESV)

OTHER PARABLES:

House built on a rock
– Matthew 7:24-27

The Weeds
– Matthew 13:24-30

Laborers in the vineyard
– Matthew 20:1-16

The Talents
– Matthew 25:14-30 and Luke 19:11-27

The Lost Sheep
– Matthew 18:10-14 and Luke 15:4-7

JESUS THE MESSIAH

In the Old Testament, the Messiah was described as the future anointed King, who was to come and bring salvation to the people of Israel and to the whole world. When Jesus came into the world and proclaimed that he was the Messiah, many did not believe him. Many were looking for a powerful soldier to remove the Romans from the land or a strong ruler who would take control of the country. Instead, Jesus came as a servant and travelled around the land talking to common people, telling parables, and healing the sick. Ultimately, those who knew Jesus and listened to him could not deny that he was the Messiah because of the miracles that he performed and the prophecies from the Old Testament that he fulfilled in his life.

This was Jesus' first recorded miracle. He and his disciples were attending a wedding, and the host ran out of wine. In Bible times, a wedding celebration could go on for a week or more, and to run out of wine was a disgrace! Mary asked Jesus to help because she knew that he had the power to do something. Mary told the servants to do whatever Jesus said. Jesus told the servants to fill six stone jars with water, then draw some out and take it to the head of the banquet. The servants did all he said, and when the head of the banquet tasted the water that had been turned into wine, he called the bridegroom aside and said this was the best wine so far! (John 2: 1-12)

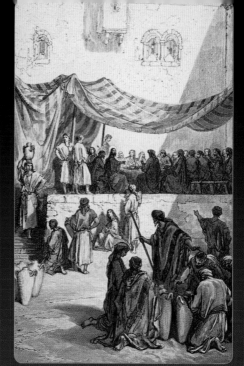

HE OFTEN DOES GO ON AND ON...

YEAH, WE KNOW.

BUT IN THIS CASE, I WOULDN'T MIND. I'D LOVE TO HEAR ABOUT ALL OF JESUS' MIRACLES!

DID JESUS EVER PULL A NICKEL OUT OF SOMEONE'S EAR? UNCLE GEORGE CAN DO THAT.

JESUS CALMS THE STORM

Once when Jesus and his disciples were travelling in a boat, Jesus was sleeping when a furious storm suddenly blew on the lake. The disciples cried for Jesus to save them, and Jesus rebuked the winds and the waves until it was completely calm. (Matthew 8:23-27)

JESUS HEALS A BLIND MAN

Jesus and his disciples passed a man who had been blind since birth. Jesus stopped, spat on the ground, and made some mud that he applied to the blind man's eyes. Then he told the man to go wash in the pool at Siloam. The man did as Jesus had told him and when he washed the mud off he could see again. The people who observed this were stunned because they had known that the man had been blind all of his life. (John 9:1-12)

JESUS CASTS OUT DEMONS

Jesus and his disciples arrived in a region called Gerasenes where they encountered two demon-possessed men. These men knew who Jesus was and asked if he had come to torment them. Jesus told the demons to leave the two men. The demons did so and were thrown into the herd of pigs nearby. Immediately, the pigs ran off a cliff and all the people who had seen the incident went to tell their friends and family. (Matthew 8:28-34)

THE FIVE THOUSAND PEOPLE

Many people had heard about Jesus and his miracles and came to see him. He drew large crowds of people who sometimes travelled great distances. On one occasion, Jesus told the disciples to find food to feed the few thousand people who had been listening to him teach that day and were hungry. The disciples told Jesus that it would cost a lot of money to feed all the people, because all they could find was a boy who had five loaves of bread and two fish. Jesus asked the disciples to bring the food to him. Jesus prayed over the small amount of food, then told the disciples to pass it out to the people. It was a miracle because after everyone had eaten, the disciples gathered up twelve baskets of broken pieces of bread and fish that were leftover. (Mark 6:33-44)

JESUS HEALS A LAME MAN

In Jerusalem, Jesus met a man who was lame from birth. Jesus asked the man, "do you wish to be healed?" Then Jesus said, "Get up! Pick up your mat and walk." Immediately the man did as he was commanded and stood up, picked up his mat and walked. (John 5:1-15)

JESUS HEALS A MAN'S HAND

Many of the religious leaders were concerned about Jesus and his ministry. When they encountered him, they would ask him questions to try and see if he would stumble and say something incorrect so they could criticize him. One day Jesus was at the synagogue and noticed a man's hand was deformed. Jesus told the man to "stretch out your hand" and the hand was instantly restored to normal. Jesus went outside and continued to heal other people who had come to see him. The religious leaders discussed this incident and became disturbed at his growing notoriety. (Matthew 12:9-14)

TEN LEPERS HEALED

Jesus travelled to many places around the country to speak with the people. One day while speaking, he shared a story about some lepers he encountered on a journey. On his way to Jerusalem, somewhere on the road between Samaria and Galilee, he passed a village where he spotted ten lepers. Jesus spoke to them and said, "Go, show yourselves to the priests." These men all did as they were told and went to the priests. Along the way, a miracle happened and they were all healed. However only one of these men came back to give thanks for the blessing he had received. Jesus asked where were the others who had been healed? Jesus asked the man, "Were not all ten cleansed? Where are the other nine? Has no one returned to give praise to God except this foreigner?" Then Jesus said to him, "Rise and go; your faith has made you well." (Luke 17:11-19)

JESUS HEALS A DEMON-POSSESSED BOY

As Jesus' disciples, they wanted to participate in his ministry. A man whose son was demon-possessed came to the disciples to ask for healing for his son, but they were unable to heal him. The man then went directly to Jesus, saying, "Lord, have mercy on my son. He has seizures and is suffering greatly … I brought him to your disciples, but they could not heal him." Jesus rebuked the demon and it came out at once. The disciples were confused about how they could not drive out the demon, and Jesus told them they needed to have more faith. (Matthew 17:14-23)

WHAT JESUS TAUGHT

One of the more famous teachings of Jesus is called the Sermon on the Mount. It is found in Matthew 5-7, and Luke 6. It is the longest of sermons, or teachings, in the gospels and covers a variety of topics from giving tithes to fasting to how to pray. In many ways, the Sermon on the Mount reminds the people of Israel about how God wants his followers to live. Jesus says that the laws of God were not to be taken as a simple statement to obey, but as truths that affect every area of life. For example, Jesus said that it's not enough to just not kill someone, but that we are not to even think bad thoughts about other people. God is interested in what is in our heart as much as what we do with our bodies.

THE SERMON ON THE MOUNT:

The Sermon on the Mount, also known as The Beatitudes, is one of Jesus' most famous teachings. Jesus said:

"Blessed are the poor in spirit, for theirs is the kingdom of heaven. Blessed are those who mourn, for they will be comforted. Blessed are the meek, for they will inherit the earth. Blessed are those who hunger and thirst for righteousness, for they will be filled. Blessed are the merciful, for they will be shown mercy. Blessed are the pure in heart, for they will see God. Blessed are the peacemakers, for they will be called children of God. Blessed are those who are persecuted because of righteousness, for theirs is the kingdom of heaven. Blessed are you when people insult you, persecute you and falsely say all kinds of evil against you because of me. Rejoice and be glad, because great is your reward in heaven, for in the same way they persecuted the prophets who were before you."

(Matthew 5:3-12)

THE LORD'S PRAYER

Regarding prayer, Jesus taught the people to pray, by giving them a model prayer to follow. Jesus said that when we pray we are to pray in the following way:

Our Father in heaven, hallowed be your name. Your kingdom come, your will be done, on earth as it is in heaven. Give us this day our daily bread, and forgive us our debts, as we also have forgiven our debtors. And lead us not into temptation, but deliver us from evil.

ADVENTURE READINGS

Jesus is rejected in his hometown Nazareth: Luke 4:14-30

Jesus teaches Nicodemus: John 3:1-21

Jesus and a Samaritan woman: John 4:4-42

Eating with sinners and tax collectors: Matthew 9:9-13

Is Jesus really Christ (the Messiah): Matthew 16:13-20

The Transfiguration: Luke 9:28-36

Who is the greatest?: Mark 9:33-37

Mary and Martha: Luke 10:38-42

The little children and Jesus: Mark 10:13-16

The rich young man: Mark 10:17-22

Little Zacchaeus: Luke 19:1-10

The greatest commandment: Mark 12:28-34

The widow's offering: Mark 12:41-44

JESUS AND THE PHARISEES

The Pharisees were a very strict group of Jews who desired to live out the laws and commandments of God in their everyday lives. While their intentions were good, to live for God every day, over time they became arrogant and began to think of themselves as better than others who didn't do what they did. Because of their position as leaders in the Jewish faith they began to gain great power in Israel.

When Jesus started to teach, much of what he said challenged their way of life. Jesus was more concerned with people's hearts than with following a set of rules out of habit. When the people started following Jesus, the Pharisees felt threatened and were afraid they would lose the respect of the people and their political power.

It wasn't long until the Pharisees were trying to discredit Jesus and get the people to turn away from him. Eventually, the Pharisees wanted to have Jesus killed because they could not refute his teaching.

PHARISEE FACTOIDS:

• Pharisees wore little boxes on their foreheads and on their arms that contained verses from Exodus and Deuteronomy.

• The Pharisees believed in resurrection, but the Sadducees didn't. That's why they were so sad, you see!

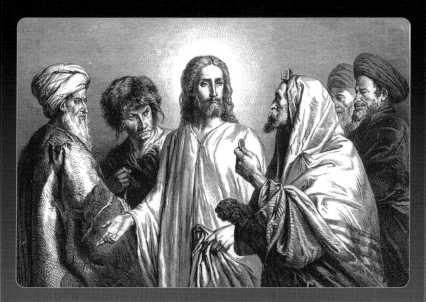

JESUS AND THE MONEY CHANGERS

During one of Jesus' visits to the temple, he noticed the tables of moneychangers and various people selling different items for sacrifice to those who were going in to worship. Jesus became angry that the area just outside of the temple was being used by some as a market place to make money. He overturned the tables and chairs, and ran the sellers away from the temple. Jesus then reminded the people that the temple was a place of worship and prayer, not a place to make money off others. Those around him listened to the words Jesus spoke. The chief priests and scribes were upset at what Jesus had done and began to plot how to kill Jesus.

THE PHARISEES TRY TO TRICK JESUS

The Pharisees wanted to trick Jesus into saying something they could use against him and ruin his image among his followers. They decided to ask him a question about paying Caesar the tax that he required from the people. The Pharisees came to Jesus and asked, "Is it right to pay taxes to Caesar or not?" Jesus knew what the Pharisees were up to and told them to show him a coin. After they gave him a coin, he held it up and asked, "Whose image and name are on this coin?" They replied that the likeness on the coin was Caesar's. Jesus responded, "Then render to Caesar the things that are Caesar's, and give to God the things that are God's." The Pharisees did not know how to reply to this answer and went away. **(Matthew 22:15-22, NCV)**

THE LAST SUPPER

Jesus and the disciples had gathered together to celebrate the Passover meal one last time. While they were eating, Jesus explained that one of the disciples would soon betray him. All of the disciples were upset and asked if they were the one who would betray him.

When the Passover meal was over, Jesus broke some unleavened bread and instructed his disciples to remember his words, "This is my body, which is for you; do this in remembrance of me." He then took a cup of wine and said, "This cup is the new covenant in my blood; do this whenever you drink it, in remembrance of me." From that day onward the church has celebrated the Lord's Supper by partaking of bread and drinking from the cup. It is an observance Jesus commanded his followers to do. (I Corinthians 11:24-25)

PASSOVER

The Passover, or what is also called the Feast of Unleavened Bread, is a seven day celebration that occurs in the spring and was given to the Jewish people to remember how God delivered them from Egypt. If you remember, the last plague that occurred in Egypt killed the firstborn son of each family who had not placed blood on the doorpost of their homes. (Exodus 12) In New Testament times, people from all over Palestine would journey to Jerusalem to participate in the Passover.

Part of the celebration for Passover includes the Seder meal, which is usually served on the first evening of Passover week. Unleavened bread is used to symbolize the fact that the slaves who escaped Egypt did not have time to bake bread with leaven in it.

WELL, ALL ALONG JESUS HAS BEEN TELLING THEM THAT HE WILL SUFFER, DIE, AND THEN COME BACK TO LIFE ON THE THIRD DAY. BUT THEY DON'T REALLY SEEM TO BELIEVE HIM.

THEY'RE GOING TO FIND OUT SOON THAT HE WAS TELLING THE TRUTH, AREN'T THEY?

YES, THEY WILL.

JESUS IS ARRESTED

Not long after the Passover meal was over, Jesus went to the Garden of Gethsemane, where he and the disciples often went to pray. All of the disciples stayed at the gate except for Peter, James, and John, who followed Jesus into the garden. There, they prayed together.

As Jesus and his disciples were leaving the garden, Judas came up with several soldiers and priests. Judas gave a signal to the guards by kissing Jesus on the cheek. Jesus was arrested and taken to the house of the High Priest to be judged.

JUDAS BETRAYS JESUS

Judas, a disciple, had been with Jesus for three years but never really understood him or his teachings. Judas believed, like most people, that Jesus was there to get rid of the Romans and to make Israel its own country again. However, Jesus was not there to do those things.

Judas was approached by the Pharisees and was paid thirty silver coins to tell them when and where they could find Jesus alone or with only a small group of people. Judas agreed and was paid the sum of money. Later, Judas led the Pharisees to the Garden of Gethsemane where Jesus was arrested.

After Jesus was crucified, Judas felt guilty because of his part in Jesus' betrayal and gave the money back to the Pharisees before he committed suicide.

JESUS ON TRIAL

Jesus was arrested and taken to Caiaphas, the High Priest. The Sanhedrin council questioned Jesus, trying to find a reason to kill him. After several questions, Caiaphas asked Jesus if he was the Son of God. Jesus answered, "I am the Son of Man." The high priest tore his clothes, which was a sign of anger, and declared to the people in the room that Jesus had committed blasphemy. At that, the council condemned Jesus to death.

Caiaphas took Jesus to Pontius Pilate, who was the governor of the Judea, Samaria, and Idumaea regions. Pilate asked Caiaphas why he didn't try Jesus himself. The reason was because the Jewish religious leaders wanted to have Jesus killed and only the Romans had the ability to sentence someone to death.

So Pilate summoned Jesus for further questioning. Jesus was accused of turning the people against the Romans, encouraging them to not pay taxes to Caesar, and calling himself a king. After Pilate talked with Jesus, he did not believe Jesus was guilty of any crime that should sentence him to death. Pilate wanted to free Jesus but was unable to due to the pressure being put on him by the Jewish leaders. Pilate decided to send Jesus to King Herod, who was in control of the surrounding jurisdiction and let him handle the matter. (John 18:29-38 and Luke 23:1-7)

THIS TRIAL IS A JOKE. THOSE WITNESSES ARE ALL LYING!

DON'T WORRY. THE TRUTH WILL COME OUT EVENTUALLY. TRUTH ALWAYS WINS IN THE END.

BUT WHAT ABOUT NOW? IF THEY LISTEN TO THESE PEOPLE, JESUS IS GOING TO BE FOUND GUILTY FOR NO REASON!

JESUS WILL TELL THE TRUTH, WON'T HE?

HE SURE WILL. THE PROBLEM IS, THEY WON'T BELIEVE HIM. AND THEY'LL FIND HIM GUILTY OF TELLING A TERRIBLE LIE.

JESUS BEFORE HEROD

King Herod welcomed the opportunity to meet with Jesus because he had heard so much about him. Herod asked Jesus many questions, but Jesus did not respond. Finally, Herod began mocking Jesus and had him dressed in an expensive robe before sending him back to Pilate. Pilate still did not want to condemn Jesus but the Jewish leaders were very insistent. (Luke 23:8-12)

CHOICE OF THE PEOPLE

According to local custom, during Passover the governor, who was Pontius Pilate at this time, could forgive a prisoner sentenced to death. Pilate announced to the Jewish people that he would be willing to release Jesus or Barabbas, who was a known criminal. At the leading of the religious leaders, the crowd chose to release Barabbas instead of Jesus. The people cried out to Pilate regarding Jesus, "Crucify him!"

Jesus was returned to prison where the Roman soldiers made a crown out of thorns and placed it on his head. They then began mocking Jesus saying, "Hail, King of the Jews."
(Matthew 27:11-32)

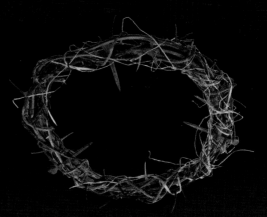

THE CRUCIFIXION

Crucifixion was a horrible way for a person to die. It had been invented by the Romans as a way to make criminals suffer before they died. A person who was crucified could live from several hours to a few days and were in extreme pain until they died.

After being arrested, mocked, and beaten, Jesus was made to carry his heavy wooden cross through Jerusalem. At one point Jesus fell and the Roman guard chose Simon of Cyrene from the crowd to continue carrying the cross to a hill called The Skull, or Golgotha.

When they arrived at Golgotha, the Roman soldiers nailed Jesus' hands and feet to the cross. He was crucified between two other men who were known robbers. The soldiers placed a sign above Jesus' head that read "Jesus, King of the Jews." The sign was written in three different languages so all could read it. After a while, Jesus cried out in a loud voice, "It is finished!" Then he died. Jesus had taken the judgment of God upon himself for all mankind. He knew that through his death he was saving the world from their sins. (Luke 23: 26-49)

THE BURIAL

Because the Sabbath was rapidly approaching, after he had died, Jesus' body was quickly prepared for burial. The body was placed in a tomb that was provided by Joseph of Arimathea, a disciple of Jesus. The soldiers placed Jesus' body in the tomb and rolled a large stone in front of the door opening. A seal was then placed on the door so that no one could move the stone without it being noticed. The Romans did not want anyone to steal Jesus' body, so they also put a unit of guards in front of the entrance. (Matthew 27:57-66)

I CAN'T BELIEVE IT. JESUS IS DEAD AND BURIED. HE'S GONE!

THE DISCIPLES MUST BE CRUSHED. ALL THEIR HOPES AND DREAMS HAVE COME TO NOTHING.

AND THEY MUST BE SO SCARED. THEY'RE PROBABLY AFRAID THEY'LL BE KILLED NEXT.

DON'T ANY OF THEM REMEMBER THAT JESUS SAID HE WOULD COME BACK TO LIFE?

IT LOOKS LIKE THEY'VE ALL FORGOTTEN ABOUT THAT.

WAIT A MINUTE. JESUS SAID HE'D COME BACK ON THE THIRD DAY. LET'S JUMP AHEAD AND SEE!

OKAY, HERE WE GO...

THE RESURRECTION

Jesus had previously told his disciples that when he went to Jerusalem he was going to die but be raised from the dead three days later. Jesus died on Friday, and early Sunday morning when Mary Magdalene and Mary arrived at the gravesite, they discovered that the stone had been rolled away and that Jesus' body was gone. To their surprise, an angel appeared to them and said, "Do not be afraid . . . He is not here, for He has risen." The angel instructed the women to tell Peter and the other disciples to go to Galilee where Jesus would meet them. (Matthew 28: 1-7 and Mark 16:1-13, ESV)

JESUS APPEARS

During the following weeks, Jesus appeared to several people. Each time, Jesus questioned the individuals about why they were sad and they would explain that it was because Jesus had died. He would then ask them about what Jesus had taught and the people would suddenly recognize him as Jesus, and that he had risen from the dead. They then went out to share with others the good news that Christ was alive.

With each appearance, Jesus proved that he was indeed the Messiah who had conquered death by rising from the dead, just as he had promised. (Luke 24:13-49 and John 21:1-14)

THERE HE IS!

OH, IT'S SO GOOD TO SEE HIM AGAIN!

IF YOU THINK WE'RE HAPPY TO SEE JESUS, JUST LOOK AT HOW HAPPY PETER AND THE REST OF THE DISCIPLES ARE.

BUT HOW DO THEY KNOW THEY'RE NOT JUST SEEING A GHOST OR A VISION?

ARE YOU KIDDING? JESUS DOESN'T ONLY SHOW HIMSELF TO THEM. HE TALKS TO THEM, LETS THEM TOUCH HIM, AND EVEN EATS WITH THEM. GHOSTS AND VISIONS CAN'T DO THAT!

THE ASCENSION

After Jesus had met with the disciples he led the disciples, outside the city of Jerusalem. Here he told the disciples that the Holy Spirit would soon come to help them while he returned to Heaven. Jesus wanted his followers to be witnesses about what Jesus had done. The book of Acts tells us that as the disciples looked on, Jesus was taken up into the clouds. The disciples watched until he vanished into the heavens, then they went back into Jerusalem to wait for the Holy Spirit. (Luke 24:50-53 and Acts 1:9-11)

JESUS IS LEAVING? SO SOON?

BUT WHY?

I KNOW IT SEEMS LIKE HE JUST CAME BACK, BUT IT'S BEEN FORTY DAYS SINCE HE ROSE FROM THE DEAD. HE'S BEEN APPEARING TO MANY PEOPLE, PROVING THAT HE'S ALIVE. NOW IT'S TIME FOR HIM TO RETURN TO HEAVEN.

HE TOLD HIS DISCIPLES HE NEEDED TO LEAVE SO THE HOLY SPIRIT COULD COME. GOD WANTS TO SEND HIS SPIRIT TO BE WITH EVERYONE WHO BELIEVES IN JESUS, INCLUDING PEOPLE IN OUR OWN TIME.

PENTECOST–THE CHURCH BEGINS

Fifty days after Passover, when the disciples had gathered to celebrate the Last Supper, they found themselves together in a room in Jerusalem waiting for the Holy Spirit, whom Jesus promised to send. Suddenly, there was the sound of a mighty rushing wind all around and tongues of fire rested on each person in the room. This was the event that was prophesied in the Old Testament concerning the Holy Spirit filling and equipping each person to tell others about Jesus Christ. After the Holy Spirit had descended, those who had been in the room went out into the community and began sharing their faith in Jesus Christ with others who would also become followers of Jesus. (Acts 2:1-13)

THE CHURCH

The word "church" refers to all people who have accepted Jesus as Savior throughout history. The church began to grow after the coming of the Holy Spirit, when Peter started preaching about Jesus and his resurrection. As a result, many gathered to hear the good news and stayed to eat together. As more people joined the group, various needs were discovered and provided for. Believers prayed together and shared their testimonies with each other. In addition to the fellowship that was experienced by all of the believers, there were also many miracles that were being performed.

Of course, the Jewish religious leaders were not happy that all of these wonderful things were happening. They wanted to eliminate anything that had to do with Jesus. The leaders thought that when they had Jesus crucified, his followers would cease to exist, but now the disciples and others who heard the gospel were spreading the news of Jesus' resurrection even more.

STEPHEN

As the church began to grow and add new people, they found that their greatest opposition was the Jewish religious leaders who were still angry with the followers of Christ. In fact, whenever possible, the Jewish leaders would have Christians falsely accused of blasphemy. Stephen was one of the men who were accused simply because they were followers of Christ. Stephen was taken outside the city and stoned to death. Stephen died still proclaiming his faith. Interestingly, the person in charge of this horrible act was a young Jewish leader named Saul, who would later become a famous follower of Christ.

PETER AND CORNELIUS

Cornelius was a guard in the Roman army and was a believer who prayed to God. One day an angel of God visited him in a vision and told him to send for Peter. Cornelius sent his servants to find Peter, who was in Joppa. Meanwhile, while the servants were traveling to Joppa, Peter was on a rooftop praying when he fell into a trance. In the trance, he had a vision of a large sheet coming down from heaven holding all kinds of four-footed animals, animals that crawled, and various birds.

Peter heard a voice that said, "Kill and eat." But Peter said he would not because some of the animals were not clean according to Jewish tradition. The voice came again, this time saying, "What God has cleansed, no longer consider unholy." Peter saw this vision three times. Suddenly Peter became aware that he had visitors, who invited Peter to visit Cornelius in Joppa.

The next day, Peter traveled to meet with Cornelius. Cornelius had invited all of his friends and family together to meet with Peter. When Peter arrived, he spoke with Cornelius and reminded him that even though it was against Jewish law for a Jew to meet with a foreigner, God had shown Peter in the vision that it was not His will for any man to be deemed unworthy for the gospel.

Cornelius asked Peter to teach the group that had gathered at his house about God's commandments. (Acts 10:1-33)

SAUL'S CONVERSION

In his younger days, Paul's name was Saul and he was a young Jewish leader. As a Jewish leader, he received permission to follow and arrest any Christians he found. On one occasion, when he was going to Damascus to seek out the Christians in that area, he had a unique encounter with Jesus. Saul and his soldiers were traveling along the road when a bright light shown all around them. A voice called out from Heaven asking, "Saul, Saul, why do you persecute me?" Saul immediately fell to the ground. God spoke with him and, when he arose, he found that he was blind. Saul had accepted Jesus and his name was changed to Paul. When the soldiers awoke, they led Paul into Damascus.

A short time later, a man named Ananias was called by God to meet with Paul and lay hands on his eyes. After Ananias did this, Paul's sight was restored. Paul changed his life and became a true follower of Christ. Paul preached and shared the gospel with those he came in contact with. (Acts 9:1-19)

Paul preached and shared the gospel in many areas throughout the Roman Empire. He went on mission trips, started churches, and wrote letters to encourage and give advice to churches that were dealing with various issues. Paul sought to live his life as Jesus did.

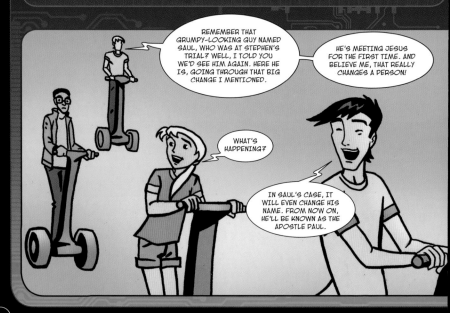

REMEMBER THAT GRUMPY-LOOKING GUY NAMED SAUL, WHO WAS AT STEPHEN'S TRIAL? WELL, I TOLD YOU WE'D SEE HIM AGAIN. HERE HE IS, GOING THROUGH THAT BIG CHANGE I MENTIONED.

HE'S MEETING JESUS FOR THE FIRST TIME. AND BELIEVE ME, THAT REALLY CHANGES A PERSON!

WHAT'S HAPPENING?

IN SAUL'S CASE, IT WILL EVEN CHANGE HIS NAME. FROM NOW ON, HE'LL BE KNOWN AS THE APOSTLE PAUL.

PAUL'S LETTERS:

Thirteen of the twenty books in the New Testament were written by Paul.

Galatians	1 & 2 Corinthians
Ephesians	Romans
Philippians	Philemon
Colossians	1 & 2 Timothy
1 & 2 Thessalonians	Titus

PAUL'S FIRST MISSIONARY TRIP

Paul's first missionary trip began in Antioch, where he and Barnabas had been ministering for about a year before God instructed the church to send the two on a missionary trip to preach the gospel. Paul and Barnabas were the first missionaries to carry the gospel to a country outside of Palestine.

The trip took about a year and half, and they traveled about 1,400 miles in all. Their trip took them to such places as Cyprus, Iconium, Lystra, and Derbe. Paul and Barnabas ministered and preached in each area, teaching about Jesus and encouraging those who believed. (Acts 13:1-12; 14:8-20)

GALATIANS

The letter to the Galatians was written to help clarify what it meant to live in the freedom that Jesus provides. Paul explained that because Jesus died for our sins, he has taken the believer's punishment on himself. As such, those who believe in Christ live a new life. He also gave the believers the fruits of the spirit, which are traits that every Christian should produce in their lives.

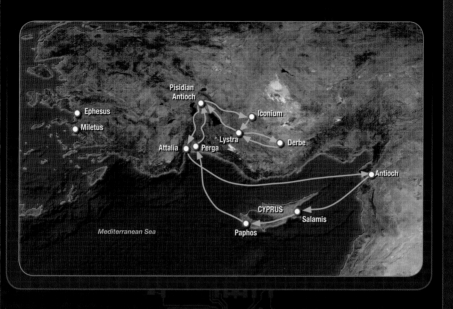

PAUL'S SECOND MISSIONARY TRIP

Paul's second missionary trip turned out to be twice as long as his first journey, covering about 2,800 miles, and it took two years to complete. Paul travelled from Antioch with Silas, through Galatia, Syria, Cilicia, and into Asia, stopping along the way to visit churches that had been established on his first trip. During this journey, Paul was joined by Timothy, a young man who would later become one of Paul's closest friends and helpers.

Paul, Silas, and Timothy then made their way to Philippi, where they encountered a slave girl who had an evil spirit that helped her predict the future. She pointed at Paul and Silas and shouted, "These men are servants of the Most High God, who are telling you the way to be saved!" And she did this every day for a long time, until Paul finally turned around and told her evil spirit, in the name of Jesus Christ, to come out of the girl. And, of course, the spirit left her. But now she couldn't make money for her owners through fortune telling, so her owners wanted revenge. They accused Paul and Silas of teaching things that went against the law.

Paul and Silas were beaten and thrown in jail, where they prayed and sang hymns. Suddenly a violent earthquake shook the building, the prison doors flew open, and everybody's chains fell off.

Under Roman law, a jailer who lost his prisoners also lost his life, so the jailer tried to kill himself rather than be executed later. But Paul stopped him. Paul didn't run away. Instead he and Silas told the jailer about Jesus, and he and his family became Christians. (Acts 16:1-40)

NEXT WE'LL BE FOLLOWING PAUL ON HIS SECOND MISSIONARY TRIP. THIS TIME HE'S TRAVELING WITH A MAN NAMED SILAS. ANOTHER YOUNG MAN, NAMED TIMOTHY, WILL JOIN THEM ALONG THE WAY. ON THIS TRIP, PAUL WILL TRAVEL MUCH FARTHER THAN HE DID ON THE FIRST ONE. ALL THE WAY TO ATHENS, GREECE!

HOW MANY OF THESE TRIPS IS HE GOING TO MAKE? I'M NOT SURE I CAN TAKE ALL THIS SEAGOING ADVENTURE.

YEAH. BUCK UP, MATE!

DON'T BE SUCH A LANDLUBBER.

1 & 2 THESSALONIANS

Paul's second missionary trip was more eventful than the first one. In Thessalonica, many people became Christians, but the Jews there started a riot and blamed Paul and Silas, so they left for Berea, where even more became believers. But the Jews from Thessalonica came to Berea and tried to start a riot again, so Paul left and went to Athens.

In these two letters to the Thessalonians, Paul reminds believers about the return of Jesus Christ. At the time, the people in Thessalonica did not understand what happens after a Christian dies. Paul explained that Jesus is coming back, and Christians will be raised back to life after Jesus returns.

After hearing Paul's message, many people got the wrong idea. They figured if Jesus was coming back, why bother working? Many quit their jobs and said, "I may as well enjoy myself until Jesus returns." Soon these people ran out of money, couldn't feed their families, and started begging from members of the church. Paul set them straight. He told them it would be a while before Jesus returned, and he told the people to go back to work, do the best you can, and be responsible while awaiting Jesus' return.

In Athens, Paul saw many statues of all kinds of gods, even an altar "to an Unknown God." Paul went up to the Areopagus, the place where all the philosophers met, and said, "I am going to tell you about that unknown God." And he preached to them about Jesus. He spoke to many people, including Stoic and Epicurean philosophers, but not too many Athenians believed Paul.

STOICS were philosophers who believed that wise people should not feel pleasure or pain.

EPICUREANS were philosophers who lived for feelings of pleasure. Their motto today would be, "If it feels good, do it!"

Once Paul and his companions reached the city of Corinth, they took some time off from traveling and stayed for a year and a half, preaching and writing letters. While in Corinth, Paul wrote his two letters to the church in Thessalonica (where the Jews had started the riots). Eventually Paul and Silas went back to Antioch where they had started their journey. (Acts 17:1-34)

PAUL'S THIRD MISSIONARY TRIP

Sometime later, Paul decided to go on another long missionary trip that would take him almost four years to complete. Though he would only travel about 2,700 miles in all, the trip lasted much longer because he ended up staying longer at each church he visited to minister and teach the people. Paul visited many churches in Galatia and Asia Minor, which is modern day Turkey. This was Paul's last trip before he was arrested and put into prison in Rome. (Acts 19:23-41; 20:7-12; 20:22-24)

EPHESIANS

In Ephesus, there was a beautiful temple for the goddess Diana (also known as Artemis). Not only were the people of Ephesus proud of their temple, they made a lot of money from people who came to visit and bought small silver models of the temple. When Paul preached about Jesus, one of the silver smiths, Demetrius, started a riot. He was afraid his business would  be ruined if people believed in Jesus. The whole city went to the theatre, and many people had no idea why they were rioting!

Paul's letter to the Ephesians was written to give encouragement and information about how to live the Christian life. Like many of the other letters Paul wrote, the letter was to be circulated among the other churches in the area. In the letter, Paul discussed the various types of religious beliefs that were infiltrating the church body. He offered guidance about prayer, living a holy life, and he also wrote about God's grace, as it is found in the gospels.

1 & 2 CORINTHIANS

The church at Corinth was a church that argued a lot, and the members had divided themselves into factions based on their favorite teacher of the Bible. In his first letter to them, Paul told them their arguing was unimportant when compared to all they had in common, especially their love of Jesus. Paul said just as your body has lots of different parts, the church also has many different kinds of people, but they all belong together in one body. (1 Corinthians 12:12-31)

He said the way for all the different people in the church to get along was simply to love each other. This letter contains the great chapter about love.

1 CORINTHIANS 13: 1-8, 13

"If I speak in the tongues of men or of angels, but do not have love, I am only a resounding gong or a clanging cymbal. If I have the gift of prophecy and can fathom all mysteries and all knowledge, and if I have a faith that can move mountains, but do not have love, I am nothing. If I give all I possess to the poor and give over my body to hardship that I may boast, but do not have love, I gain nothing.

Love is patient, love is kind. It does not envy, it does not boast, it is not proud. It does not dishonor others, it is not self-seeking, it is not easily angered; it keeps no record of wrongs. Love does not delight in evil but rejoices with the truth. It always protects, always trusts, always hopes, always perseveres.

Love never fails. ... And now these three remain: faith, hope, and love. But the greatest of these is love."

ROMANS

Rome was the capital of the Roman Empire and the largest empire the world had ever seen. In his letter to the Romans, Paul begins by reminding the church that all people are sinners and that only belief in Jesus Christ can change them. Paul shows through such examples as Adam and Abraham how the Old Testament and New Testament are tied together by the teachings of Jesus Christ. Paul then closes the letter by answering a range of questions people in the church were asking.

THE MAMERTINE PRISON: The prison where Paul supposedly spent the last years of his life.

THE COLOSSEUM: The rooms you see were under the floor of the arena. In these rooms, the gladiators, lions, and Christians waited until they had to go into the arena to fight and be killed.

AND HERE YOU HAVE IT, THE ROMAN COLOSSEUM. AS YOU KNOW, PAUL WROTE MANY LETTERS TO CHURCHES IN FARAWAY LANDS. THE BOOK OF ROMANS IS HIS LETTER TO THE CHRISTIANS HERE IN ROME.

IN THAT LETTER, PAUL SAID HE WANTED TO VISIT ROME SOMEDAY. HE DID GET TO GO, BUT NOT ON ONE OF HIS MISSIONARY TRIPS. HE ENDED UP TRAVELING TO ROME AS A PRISONER!

HOW DID THAT HAPPEN?

LET'S GO BACK IN TIME AND SEE!

I preached and shared the gospel in many areas throughout the Roman Empire. [I] went on mission trips, started churches, and wrote letters to encourage and give [adv]ice to churches that were dealing with various issues. Paul sought to live his life [as J]esus did. In the end, it was his boldness in proclaiming the gospel that led to his [arre]st and imprisonment.

[Pau]l returned to Jerusalem after his third trip, and he told the apostles and the rest [of t]he church all the great things God had done during his travels. But some Jews [saw] Paul preaching and started another uproar by falsely accusing Paul of speaking [aga]inst the Law and the temple. The crowd went wild, and Roman soldiers had to [resc]ue Paul from being killed by the mob.

[Eve]ntually, Paul was taken to the city of Caesarea and brought before the Roman [gov]ernor, Felix. Felix knew Paul was not guilty, but he didn't set Paul free. Instead, [he] kept Paul waiting—for two years. (Acts 24:24-27) While in Caesarea, Paul was [able] to preach the gospel to Roman soldiers, governors, and to King Herod Agrippa.

[Whe]n Felix was replaced by a new governor, Festus, Paul made use of his right as [a Ro]man citizen to appeal to the Roman supreme court rather than be sent back to [Jeru]salem, where he was sure to be killed. This meant that nobody except the emperor [in R]ome had the right to try Paul's case, and even though Festus and King Agrippa both [agre]ed that Paul should really be set free, it was too late. Paul had to go to Rome.

PAUL'S TRIP TO ROME

The fastest way to get to Rome was by ship, so Paul set sail on a ship across the Mediterranean Sea with his Roman guard and Luke (the doctor who wrote the gospel of Luke and the book of Acts). On the way, a storm blew the ship off course and it was smashed to pieces near an island called Malta.

Luke describes this story more in the book of Acts, but Luke may have been planning to write a third book because Paul's story ends right in the middle. All we know is that Paul was set free and made a fourth missionary journey. During this time, he wrote letters to Timothy and Titus.

After his fourth missionary journey, Paul was put back into prison in Rome, this time in a real prison, actually more like a dungeon. And there he was put to death, about thirty years after he met Jesus on the road to Damascus, and about two years before the Romans destroyed the temple in Jerusalem in AD 70.

PAUL'S LETTERS

EPHESIANS

In Ephesians, Paul talks about the wonderful things we have in Christ and tells us how we should live as Christians. He also talks to children and parents and describes the armor of God.

THE ARMOR OF GOD: EPHESIANS 6:10-17

"Finally, be strong in the Lord and in his mighty power. Put on the full armor of God, so that you can take your stand against the devil's schemes. For our struggle is not against flesh and blood, but against the rulers, against the authorities, against the powers of this dark world and against the spiritual forces of evil in the heavenly realms. Therefore put on the full armor of God, so that when the day of evil comes, you may be able to stand your ground, and after you have done everything, to stand. Stand firm then, with the belt of truth buckled around your waist, with the breastplate of righteousness in place, and with your feet fitted with the readiness that comes from the gospel of peace. In addition to all this, take up the shield of faith, with which you can extinguish all the flaming arrows of the evil one. Take the helmet of salvation and the sword of the Spirit, which is the word of God."

IN SPITE OF EVERYTHING, PAUL MADE IT TO ROME. A PRISONER, YES, BUT THAT DIDN'T STOP HIM FROM WRITING LETTERS AND TELLING PEOPLE ABOUT JESUS.

THAT'S REALLY GREAT.

GO, PAUL!

PAUL DID SOME OF HIS MOST IMPORTANT WORK WHILE HE WAS UNDER ARREST. THE LETTERS HE WROTE BECAME PART OF THE NEW TESTAMENT. AND HE SHARED THE GOSPEL WITH MANY HIGH-RANKING PEOPLE.

PHILIPPIANS

Paul wrote the letter of Philippians from a prison cell in Rome, but Paul talks more about joy in Philippians than in any other of his letters. He opens the letter by describing himself as a servant of Christ and that it was his duty in life to do the work that Jesus called him to. He tells us not to worry, but to trust God and imitate Jesus. And we should fill our minds with good things.

PHILIPPIANS 4:8-9

"Finally, brothers and sisters, whatever is true, whatever is noble, whatever is right, whatever is pure, whatever is lovely, whatever is admirable—if anything is excellent or praiseworthy—think about such things. Whatever you have learned or received or heard from me, or seen in me—put it into practice. And the God of peace will be with you."

COLOSSIANS

In Colossae there were people teaching wrong things about Jesus, so Paul wrote to remind them again that Jesus Christ is the only way to salvation, and that what he has done for us is enough! Paul also talks about Christian relationships and what it means to live as a Christian.

PHILEMON

Paul wrote the letter of Philemon to his friend, Philemon. He wrote the letter after meeting one of Philemon's slaves whose name was Onesimus. Onesimus had run away from Philemon and had become a Christian. Paul wrote Philemon asking him to forgive Onesimus and to take him back into his home. Paul also asked Philemon to take him back as a brother and not as a slave.

1 & 2 TIMOTHY

Paul wrote this letter to Timothy as a father would to a son. Its purpose was to give Timothy advice on various issues related to the ministry, such as working with church members and choosing elders to help make decisions. In his second letter, Paul warns Timothy about the increase in persecution of Christians. He also encourages Timothy to continue preaching boldly in the face of persecution, even though some may consider him "too young" and choose not to listen.

TITUS

Paul wrote this short letter to Titus regarding how to deal with individuals who cause problems in the church and how to choose leaders to help lead the church.

MORE BOOKS OF THE BIBLE

During Paul's ministry, he found himself in different prisons, which he turned into opportunities to witness to those guarding him. Like Jesus, Paul was questioned before the Sanhedrin, who wanted him sentenced to death. Thirty years after Paul became a Christian on the road to Damascus, he was put to death because of his faith.

JAMES & JUDE

It might seem like the entire New Testament was written by Paul, but many others contributed, like James and Jude. Many believe that the two brothers of Jesus wrote the books of James and Jude, which bear their names. The book of James exhorts believers to live out their faith in practical ways, whereas the book of Jude encourages believers to stand for the faith they believe.

HEBREWS

Hebrews is a book whose author is unknown. This book is written to Jewish believers who were facing persecution because of their faith and encourages believers to stay true to Jesus Christ in the face of persecution. The major theme of the book is centered around how much better the new covenant that Jesus provides in salvation is than the covenant that God gave to the Israelites through Moses. Jesus is shown to be a better high priest, a better sacrifice, and a final revelation of God to mankind.

SO THAT'S IT? THIS IS WHERE THE BIBLE ENDS, WITH PAUL IN PRISON?

Peter wrote two letters in the New Testament when he was older and much wiser in his faith. His first letter was written after the Neronian persecution of Christians. The ruler, Nero, had made it a crime for people living in Rome to be followers of Christ. They suffered horribly and were often killed. Others fled into the surrounding lands to escape the persecution. This letter encouraged Christians to remain true to the faith and reminded them of the hope in the Spirit's arrival. Peter also discussed the end times in his second letter. He gives Christians a warning to beware of false teachers that will be trying to lead them away from the truth of Jesus' teaching.

1, 2, and 3 JOHN

These three letters were written by John, a disciple of Jesus. The letters are warnings against false teachers that Christians may encounter. He also discusses how we should love one another even when it might not be easy.

198

REVELATION

The New Testament ends with a spectacular vision—and the promise that God will make all things new. The book of Revelation is the last book in the Bible, written by the apostle John while on the island of Patmos, and it contains visions that God gave to John about the last days before Jesus returns. The visions foretold some strange and disturbing images, but it ends with rejoicing because the time has come for God to make all things new! At the very end of Revelation Jesus says, "Yes, I am coming soon." And John's answer is, "Amen. Come, Lord Jesus!"

READING GUIDE TO THE BIBLE

Below you will find a listing of important passages that will guide you in reading
the Bible. You could just start at the book of Genesis and read through to the book
of Revelation, or you could use the following reading guide and discover the major
stories of the Bible for yourself and gain an overall understanding of what the Bible is
all about. So grab your Bible, start reading, and enjoy the adventure.

OLD TESTAMENT

READING GUIDE TO THE BIBLE

READING GUIDE TO THE BIBLE

READING GUIDE TO THE BIBLE

READING GUIDE TO THE BIBLE

THE APOSTLES' CREED

I believe in God

> There is only one God. In the Bible we learn that there is only one God who is expressed in three persons: the Father, the Son (Jesus), and the Holy Spirit.

the Father almighty, Creator of heaven and earth,

> God the Father is almighty (all-powerful) – no one is more powerful than God. He made the universe by himself, out of nothing, simply by speaking it into existence. He also made human beings after his own image, which makes all people special.

and in Jesus Christ, his only Son, our Lord.

> When Adam and Eve lived in the Garden of Eden, they ate the fruit from the tree that God had told them not to eat from. Because they disobeyed God, all people are now sinners and separated from God. But because God loved us, he sent his one and only Son, Jesus, into this world to save us from our sins.
>
> When we say Jesus is our Lord, we mean that he has the right to tell us what to do, and we promise to obey him.

He was conceived by the power of the Holy Spirit, and born of the Virgin Mary.

> Jesus was born into the world, which we celebrate each year at Christmas, through Mary his mother. And even though God was his father, she gave birth to him just like any mother gives birth to a baby.

He suffered under Pontius Pilate, was crucified, died, and buried. He descended to the dead. On the third day he rose again.

> Jesus taught many things about God and his kingdom while on earth, and he healed many people. But there were also many people who hated him for what he did and said. In the end, his enemies arrested him and put him on trial, even though he had never committed any sin in his entire life. Pontius Pilate, the Roman who ruled over Palestine, allowed Jesus to be condemned to death. Jesus died one of the most horrible kinds of death: death on a cross. He was crucified on Friday, was buried in a grave, and left there. Jesus died for our sins; that is, Jesus died in our place. And because of this, we no longer need to be afraid to die.
>
> On Sunday morning, however, after being in the grave for three days, Jesus came to life. He now lives forever. No one had ever done this before. Jesus proved that he was stronger than death.

He ascended into heaven, and is seated at the right hand of the Father.

> Forty days after his resurrection, Jesus went back home to be with his Father in heaven where he sits on a throne, right next to God. He is in charge of everything that is happening in the world, and he is taking care of all those who follow him.

He will come again to judge the living and the dead.

> Someday Jesus will return to this earth and when this happens, all those who have believed in him, even though they may be dead, will also rise again and go with him to heaven. All of his enemies, however, will be cast into hell.

I believe in the Holy Spirit,

> On Pentecost Sunday, Jesus sent his Spirit to the church as recorded in Acts 2. The Holy Spirit lives in us and helps us obey God's laws and his Son Jesus.

the holy Catholic church,

> If we believe in Jesus, we belong to his church. Jesus wants us to tell others about him and so increase the size of his church. "Catholic" in the Apostles' Creed does not mean "Roman Catholic" but "universal" – the church of Jesus includes all Christians everywhere and whenever they have lived, live, or will live!

the communion of saints,

> Christians everywhere should love and help one another, because we are all part of the same spiritual family.

the forgiveness of sins,

> God was angry at us because we were sinners. But because of his grace, he promises to forgive our sins if we ask Jesus to come into our hearts.

the resurrection of the body,

> When we die, our body is laid in a grave, but our spirit goes to be with Jesus. And just as Jesus rose from the dead, someday all those who have believed in him will also rise from the dead and receive new, perfect bodies.

and the life everlasting.

> When Jesus finally comes again and takes us to our home in heaven, he promises that we will live there forever and ever. We will never die again!

Amen.

> "Amen" is a Hebrew word that means something like "Yes!" When you say "amen" at the end of a prayer, you are saying "Yes! I believe that you can do this, Lord." At the end of this creed it means, "Yes! This is what I believe!"

SCRIPTURE INDEX

SCRIPTURE INDEX

SUBJECT INDEX

SUBJECT INDEX

 Pg. 19: Adam and Eve leaving the Garden of Eden, Public Domain

 Pg. 22: Ancient ziggurat, CC-BY 3.0, Hardnfast/Wikimedia Commons

  Pg. 23: Photo Disc, © William D. Mounce, Artville

  Pg. 25: Photo of a donkey and camel, © 1995 Phoenix Data Systems,

 Pg. 29: People working on the Nile River, © Angel Blanco, BigstockPhoto

 Pg. 30: Pyramids - ©1995 Phoenix Data Systems © John Campana/Flickr, Wikimedia Commons

 Pg. 30: Pyramids, © 1995 Wan Rosli Wan Othman/www.dreamstime.com

 Pg. 31: Ancient jewelry/artifacts, © John Campana/Flickr, CC-BY 2.0

 Pg. 31: Mummy, Wikimedia Commons

 Pg. 31: King Tut gold mask, © 1995 Phoenix Data Systems

 Pg. 34: Statue of Pharoah, © Kim Walton, courtesy of the Aegyptisches Museum, Berlin

IMAGE GUIDE

pg. 89: **Goats, Shutterstock**

pg. 89: **Tower of David,**
  © **Sean Parone/Alamy**

Pg. 93: **Pasture with sheep,**
  © **Todd Bolen/www.BiblePlaces.com**

Pg. 103: **King David Shutterstock**

Pg. 103: **King Solomon, Shutterstock, Public Domain**

Pg. 104-105: **Hezekiah's tunnel,**
  © **1995 Phoenix Data Systems**

Pg. 108-109: **Bullet train,**
  © **Hung Chung Chih, Shutterstock**

Pg. 113: **Statue of King Nebichadnezzar's dream,**
  © **2011 Zondervan**

Pg. 117: **"The vision of the valley of dry bones",**
Public Domain

Pg. 127: **Temple,**
  © **William D. Mounce**

Pg. 134: **Nativity scene,**
  © **Lebrecht Music and Arts Photo Library/Alamy**

Pg. 139: Jordan River,
© 1995 Phoenix Data Systems

Pg. 139: The Baptism of Christ, © Convent of San Pietro, Perugia,
1496-98, Perugino, Pietro (c.1445-1523)/Musee des Beaux-Arts,
Rouen, France/Giraudon/The Bridgeman Art Library

Pg. 147: Jesus turns water to wine, Shutterstock, Public Domain

Pg. 149: Jesus Stilling the Tempest
Public Domain

Pg. 150: "Jesus and the Blind Man," Dixon, Arthur A. (fl.1890-1927)/
Private Collection/© Look and Learn/The Bridgeman Art Library

Pg. 152: Jesus preaching to crowd, Public Domain

Pg. 155: Jesus and Parisees, Shutterstock, Public Domain

Pg. 155: Parisees, Shutterstock

Pg. 155: Prayer shawl, Shutterstock

Pg. 158-159: The Last Supper,
Public Domain

Pg. 161: Judas betraying Jesus,
Public Domain